Bradamant's Quest

"You are Bradamant, a warrior of Charlemagne," Oberon said. "I have a boon to ask of you."

She had heard of this king in Faerie. "What do you want, Majesty?"

He said gently, "It's time to give back the gifts of Faerie. If you will undertake this as a quest, you shall have honor and glory in Faerie."

...but when Bradamant took on the quest, she didn't know that her brother would think it was trafficing with devils. Her cousins the magicians didn't want to give up their carefully indexed books of magic (much less the hippogriff—a useful steed and a loyal companion). Her sister-in-law was willing to give up the spear of Galafrone, but not until she'd finished using it. And her cousin Roland seemed to be haunting his grave, where his magically enduring sword was buried with him, and dead set against being disturbed. What's a warrior to do when valor alone is not enough for her to complete a quest?

BRADAMANT'S QUEST

RUTH BERMAN

FTL PUBLICATIONS
MINNEAPOLIS, MINNESOTA

FTL Publications
P O Box 22693
Minneapolis, MN 55422-0693
www.ftlpublications.com
mail@ftlpublications.com

Cover art copyright © 2011 by Alicia Austin

Printed in the United States of America

ISBN 978-1-936881-02-4

"The Dragon's Skin" was previously published in *Dragon Fantastic*, ed. Rosalind M. & Martin H. Greenberg, NY: DAW Books, 1992.

"The Buried Sword" was previously published in *Asimov's Science Fiction*. June 2004.

In memory of my father,
Reuben Berman,
physician, musician, and encourager.

Chapter 1
The Golden Helm

"Is Renald come home?" King Charlemagne asked.

Bradamant looked at him in surprise. Surely any message bringing news of her brother's whereabouts would have been delivered to their uncle both as kinsman and as King of France, as well as to her. The victory celebrations, such as they were, and the mourning days for the dead were mostly complete, but the celebrations had not much lightened the mourning for either of them.

He stopped beside her under a high archway, striped brightly with red and yellow stone facing. Beyond, in a hall of the palace, Prince Charlot and Prince Louis were playing chess. The boys had not been with them at the battle at Roncesval. They played their game intently.

After the battle, Bradamant had sent her soldiers home to Este, and with them the message to her son that he was now the lord of Este. Her husband Roger was one of the many who had died in winning safe passage for the French back from Spain into France and securing the border between them. She had stayed with the king and the rest of the army as they marched slowly from Roncesval to Paris. The loss of her cousin Roland, the king's chief warrior as well as his nephew, and so many others of her fellow warriors, was hard for all the survivors. From Paris they had returned to Aix-la-Chapelle, the empire's capital, where the king disbanded the foot-soldiers not already sent to their homes.

Bradamant stopped herself from sighing and told him, "I haven't had any news. I suppose he could be." It was bitter to think that her brother had been still journeying on pilgrimage in his exile during the fighting. Not that it would have made any difference if Renald had been at Roncesval. He would have died with her husband and the king's nephew Roland and the rest of the Peers and the others in the rear-guard, that was all. Even Roland's magically enduring sword, Durendal, had not saved any lives in the rear-guard. "I could go to Renald's castle at Montalban and see if they've heard anything of him."

The king nodded and looked down, twisting his gold seal-ring, with its double-headed eagle, the sign of commanding power for the French now, as for the Romans and the Trojans before them. Her husband Roger had borne an eagle for his emblem, too.

Bradamant took her leave and set off for Montalban.

The trees were still bare. Poplars lined the road, the grey trunks and the tall white branches flashing silver where the sun lit them. A small patch of snow lay north of each one, shining against the darkness of the muddy ground, a light that marked the absence of sunlight. There was no grass yet, except where the ground sloped south. The footing was not as good as it might have been, for the roads were still wet. But Marron was a strong horse, if not quite as strong as his sire, Bayard, and he made good time.

When she came into the forests of the Ardennes, poplars gave way to thick groves of oak and chestnut. Even without new leaves, the heavy branches shut out much of the sky.

When she came over a ridge and saw a stream running along the bottom of the valley there, she thought it was time for Marron to have some water, but the water at the ford was muddy. She dismounted and led Marron upstream, walking noisily, so as not to surprise any stray wolf or boar. The king hunted in these woods, and, given warning, all the animals would avoid a human step. She caught one glimpse of a weasel, staring at her from under a bramble bush. The little eyes glittered, and then it spun about silently and disappeared down a tunnel.

When she reached water that ran almost clear, she set Marron free to drink and graze a little on the remains of last year's grasses. The bread she had brought with her was stale, but she bit and chewed doggedly to stop her stomach from rumbling.

She wrapped her cloak around her and snuggled her hands in a fold of the wool, then leaned against a tree and looked about. Some of the oaks were covered with stubborn leaves, left over from the autumn. They were copper where the light came through, black in the shadow. A single snowdrop had come into bloom and stood in a patch of mud, so white it looked like silver bells.

Bradamant blinked and squinted her eyes, trying to see it more clearly. It *was* silver—but it couldn't be, could it? The little bells began to sway, and she felt a breeze on her face. The shadows in the darkness of the oak behind the snowdrop stirred, and took shape.

A boy dressed in black robes and wearing a silver crown stood before her. No, not a boy. His body was too long and lean; his head and feet fit too well with him to be those of a child yet to finish growing, or a dwarf whose growth had ended early.

He was one of the little people.

When he began to speak she wondered if she had mistaken the appearance of things. His voice was soft, as if from far away—perhaps he was, and it was only distance that made him seem small.

No. His words were distinct, and, anyway, how could he be farther off than the trunk of the oak tree behind him?

"You are Bradamant, a warrior of Charlemagne," he said.

She crossed herself, but nothing happened, except that he laughed.

"I have a boon to ask of you," he said.

"What are you?"

"I am called Oberon."

She had heard of this king in Faerie. She crossed herself again, still without result. The priests most often said the fays were devils, but then they also said that her cousin Malgis was damned because he was a magician, and that seemed to her unlikely. Her cousin Astolf was a magician, too, after all, and no one called him a lost soul. Of course, he was English, and expected to be odd. Perhaps the little people were like the paynim, with damned souls but as much ordinary good and evil, and as much worldly honesty as other people had. Humans were like that. But then it was said also that the little people had no souls. And many said that they were crafty, lying by equivocation. Everyone said that they held by their word. And it did not bother him when she crossed herself. She gave up the riddle. "What do you want, Majesty?"

But instead of answering directly, he said, "The world grows old, and it grows further from us, year by year."

This was as much of a riddle as the rest. "Do you mean to stop the world from getting old?"

"If I did, I wouldn't ask a mortal's help," said Oberon, wryly.

"Just as well. I don't think I'd be much good at it."

He said gently, "It's time to give back the gifts of Faerie. They're too powerful for mortals to use safely—and they lose, in your world, by little and little, those powers which they have and draw from us. We grow the weaker in their failure."

"But if the Spanish attack again—"

"You are both weary of fighting." Oberon raised his head up and to the side for a moment, as if trying to imagine the future or to see into it. Then he fixed his grey eyes on her again and said, "It's hard to know if gifts of power bring victory more swiftly or serve only to kill mortals in larger numbers. Your cousin Roland threw the Frisian king's fire engine into the North Sea rather than leave so dangerous a weapon in the world."

Well, that was true enough. Bradamant rested her hand on her sword, not to draw it, but to feel the comforting solidity and smoothness of the ruby in the hilt. "Majesty," she said, "this would be a work of many years. The journey to Far Cathay alone would—"

"Cathay? Oh—you mean the Princess Angelica's ring of invisibility. No. Such talismans I leave to others. I ask of you only the gifts you have yourself, in your own family."

"I? But I have nothing!" She caught her hand away from the sword and looked down at it, half fearing to see hell-flames burst magically from it. It was still only her old, familiar sword, made for her by her father's armorer.

"Where is the lance from Cathay your cousin Astolf gave you?"

"But that isn't magic—it's only lucky." Bradamant listened to her own words and was astonished. "I thought it was my own skill," she said ruefully.

"Your skill is considerable," said Oberon, "but as you say, there is luck in the spear. Old Galafrone had the tempering of it beyond the world."

"But I don't have it. I gave it to Marfisa, my sister—Roger's sister—and she's gone off wandering since we avenged Roger's death."

"You are generous," he said dryly. "Your cousin Roland's sword, Durendal?"

"We buried it with him at Roncesval."

"And what did you do with the shield your husband won from the magician Atlante?"

"Roger threw it away so that no one would be tempted to use so dishonorable a device."

Oberon was evidently starting to find this litany amusing. He managed not to smile at the carelessness of mortal generosity, but his eyes and brows were alive with mischief. "Surely your husband won the dragonskin armor of Nimrod when he defeated Rodomont in tourney?"

"Oh, so that's why the mail looked just like scales!"

Oberon waited patiently.

"No. Rodomont wore fresh armor to fight Roger. I won his mail by the grave of Isabel of Galicia—but I buried it there in the shrine."

"Of course. And the golden helmet of Mambrino, which your brother won?"

"I don't know if Renald left it at Montalban or took it with him into exile."

"Astolf's hippogriff?"

"He set him free." She thought a moment and added, "But I don't know if he went home. He liked Astolf."

"What of the book to undo spells and the olifant Logistilla gave him?"

"I don't know—the horn lost its power in the Moon."

"The book of spells your cousin Malgis uses for his sorcery?"

"Oh, yes, he has that."

"A wonder!" said Oberon.

"—but I don't think he'd ever let it go."

"Well, well. It would seem, Bradamant, that I am asking a quest more difficult than I knew. But will you undertake it?"

"What can I gain?"

Oberon stooped and picked up a brown oakleaf. He blew on it, and it turned to gold. The sharp curves of the indentations flashed, catching what light there was. He tossed it to her, and she caught the brightness in her hands. She had expected something as light as a leaf, and had to take a step to catch her balance. It was as heavy as gold.

"Fairy gold is little worth," he said. "This is a pretty gaud if you will keep it from the touch of cold iron. But gauds, I think, are all I can give you. I must retrieve talismans of power now, and not bestow them. If you will undertake this as a quest, you shall have honor and glory in Faerie."

Bradamant's father, Duke Aymon, was as proud as he was stubborn, and all his children had taken from him the longing for glory. But— "Could you bring Roger back to life?" she said.

"No. I could make you an airy likeness of him. You might find it a comfort in your bed, and it could talk with you in his voice, but its words would come only from your memories."

Bradamant shook her head. She would like to hear Roger's voice again, even if all it had to say was things he'd said before. But Oberon seemed to think it would be cheating of some sort, and maybe he was right. "No. Let it be fame. I'll try to find the things for that—it's better than a ghost."

"Is it?" said Oberon. "Then I thank you. Call me in any place of old powers, when you have a talisman to return to me, and I'll meet you there."

Bradamant looked at him doubtfully, worried again by his mention of unhuman powers.

Oberon shook his head, guessing her fear. "The old powers were not devils," he said. "They were more powerful than your people commonly are, that's all. I can hear you from their places. But if you fear them—" He held out his hand for her to give him back the gold leaf.

His willingness to take no for an answer added a good deal to her comfort. She did not think Oberon could mean more ill by her than an evil human might have done, and she was a fair judge of humans. She could be deceived—she had been before—but not often. She thought Oberon meant well by her, and if she could trust him that far, she ought to be able to trust his judgment of the others like him. There were priests, she knew, who fumed mightily when a maid so much as dropped a coin down a wishing well to wish for a lover. Some wishing wells were dangerous enough. But that was because love was dangerous. She had never thought the wishing damnable.

"I'll try," she said. She tucked the gold oakleaf into the width of a sleeve and stooped to gather up the flower. The stem broke easily, and Bradamant put the silver spray in the other sleeve. Gold and silver prickled a moment against her arms, but then she forgot them. Oberon was shrinking. The breeze was up again, blowing on her back. He grew small, and smaller, and vanished. The wind sang for a moment in the branches of the trees, and then it was gone.

Bradamant looked about her. To one side, away from the river, she heard water bubbling. She went after the sound and came to a pair of springs, each banked around with earth, and the earth tiled with mosaics, apparently long untended, for both were overgrown with moss. Bradamant sat down on one, but Oberon's voice, so soft it was hardly more than a thought, said, "I wouldn't, if I were you." Bradamant jumped up, looked at the moss, then set to work pulling enough of it off to let her see the patterns.

Each fountain showed a winged boy, much faded and discolored, but clear enough in outline. Each held a bow and arrows. She could no longer tell which was armed with gold and which with ebon, but it scarcely mattered to her which was Eros and which Anteros. She had no mind to fall into a passion, either of love or hatred, with the next person she met. Her brother Renald had had trouble enough, loving Angelica, and all for an unwary drink of water. And while he'd been at it, Angelica's heart was set on leaving these mad Franks behind and winning her way home across the world to Cathay.

Renald's wife Clarice had not been well pleased, either.

Bradamant had thought to fill up her wine-skins with water, to stretch out her supply of drink, but it could wait. She bowed to the air and said, in case Oberon still had the corner of his eye on her, "Thanks, my lord," then made her way out of the grove of old powers.

From Paris she followed the old Roman roads that zig-zagged south, up the Seine and overland to the Loire, then around the edges of the Central Massif, and so home. Charlemagne had been prodding his nobles to build more roads, but the work took time.

In the south the poplars along the road gave way to olives, bright with the clusters of little white flowers among the grey-green leaves. The undersides of the leaves were rimy white, and as breezes tossed them up or down the olives glimmered light and dark.

Reluctantly, Bradamant unpacked her armor. She did not expect to need it, but it was not so long since they had fought Saracens up and down this countryside. So it was back to the routine of stuffing herself into her gear each morning—mailshirt and leggings, gloves and helm. Armor and arms together were worth over 30 cows—enough to stock a royal estate.

Dealing with armor took time, as always, but now, besides that, she found at the end of a day's riding cased in iron and leather that her legs were swollen. It was hard to get them out of the greaves, and her feet were so sore that it was painful to walk even as far as behind a bush. An old woman, she decided, that's what she was. She shouldn't be going on a quest, she should be at home at Este telling the boy how to manage the estate. Not that he'd appreciate it, and she didn't like calling herself too old to do what she said she would. Everyone knew Duke Aymon's brood were stubborn. And she wasn't all that old, either. She still timed her journeys, when practical, so that she would not be on the road when beginning her month. She intended to reach Montalban before the next.

When she came in sight of her brother's castle of Montalban, the mountain was as white as its name, the meadows sudsy with anemones. They rippled in the breeze, like foam on water. Marron trotted faster, seeing a familiar place with the promise of oats.

Across the field a warrior on a grey horse, seeing their charge uphill, lowered his lance and came riding at them.

Bradamant's first thought was so well drilled into her arms and legs that she had put it into action for some time before going on to her second thought.

The first thought was defense. She wheeled Marron to the side, and touched her heels to his flanks to start the gallop, brought her lance out of its rest and aimed it with one hand, and swung up her shield with the other.

Meanwhile, her second thought had taken shape at the sight of her enemy's boots tucked firmly in the stirrups, the better to ride her down without being unseated himself.

Not all of Charlemagne's warriors were so comfortable riding full tilt to collision. And that particular line of arm and shoulder to lance was familiar—Bradamant had seen it since they were children jousting on hobby horses, with mullein stalks for spears.

She wheeled again to let the charge go past her, set the lance at rest, and took off her helmet. Her hair was darker now than in earlier days. It fell down about her shoulders, brown instead of fair.

Renald circled round, shouting "Coward!" and pulled up in confusion, seeing her face, framed in the long tresses.

Bradamant trotted towards him.

"If you'd keep the muck of the road off your shield," he complained, "you'd give your friends a better chance to know you."

She pointed at his own muddy shield, and he made a face at her. Then they were close enough to embrace and kiss. Even next to him, she could hardly see a gleam from the silver mountain on his shield.

They went on up, twisting back and forth across the hillside, on the road to the castle. Bradamant would have liked to delay giving him the news, but he asked after her husband, so she told him.

Renald nodded. His thin face was getting wrinkled, and the lines seemed to deepen as he heard of Roncesval. "I was afraid it must be something like that," he said. "The horse I was riding ran away with me one day, and I thought surely it was Malgis setting some cantrip to bring me home. But he forgot to think of the heat. At Acre the horse fell dead, and I found myself sick with the ague. I wasn't able to look for shipping until months later."

At the gate, once the porter looked at their dusty faces more carefully, there was a great bustle—sending for Renald's two sons, who were out helping to plough for the spring planting, sending for the steward, calling for wine and rooms and fresh clothes to be prepared, calling for someone to stable the horses, then apologizing when an older servant interrupted angrily that the lord would want to see to that himself.

"Yes, thanks, Humphrey," said Renald, and took the old man by the sleeve. "Why doesn't anyone tell me where my wife is?"

Humphrey cleared his throat and reached up to pat Renald's mailed shoulder. "I'm sorry, lad. Lady Clarice took ill this last winter—"

"Dead?"

"Yes."

Renald nodded and set out for the stable, with its comforting, familiar smells of musty hay, horseflesh, and horse droppings.

Bayard had been left behind when Renald went on his pilgrimage. The horse reared up, neighing a welcome. Renald turned aside to hug the stallion, hiding his face against the bay stallion's warm flank for a moment.

Bradamant followed, and they groomed and fed their horses in silence.

They met again at supper, cleaned, combed, and dressed in velvet robes embroidered with silk lilies. (The robes were not quite clean, but they had been carefully brushed, and Renald's steward, a thrifty soul, still considered them noble, not ready to be given to the servants.)

Bradamant was quiet during most of the meal. Renald and the boys were trying, awkwardly, to get used to each other.

It was not until Aymonet and Yonet withdrew that she told him her errand. He sat quietly, eating his sauce of dried fruits in honey, and drinking a cup of thin local wine. He made no comment, but heard her out in silence.

"Will you let me take the helmet?" she said, at the end.

"No."

"But—"

"Here I am just back from pilgrimage, and you ask me to give to devils?"

"He wasn't a devil."

"The priests say fairies—"

"The priests say devils fear the cross," she interrupted.

"The helmet's mine," he answered.

"I'll fight you for it," she said. Honor required that she do her best to gain the helm, but having done that, she could fail honorably.

"Not if I'm the only one with something to lose. What will you offer me if I win?"

Bradamant recognized the casual tone which had signaled a trap when they were both children, fox that he was. They should really have called him Renard. He'd even had the red hair, back then. But there didn't seem to be any way to keep her word to Oberon without springing Renald's trap. Besides, she wanted to find out what it was. "What would you suggest?"

"If you lose, you give up your devil's quest."

Snap! she said to herself. It made an interesting point of honor: was it better to give up the helmet of Mambrino and continue the remainder of the quest, or should she stand fast and try for all? Renald was certainly the better fighter, unless he was slowing with age. She looked at his hands, but saw no swelling in the knuckle joints to suggest that he was beginning to have any trouble with inflammation in his bones. She would have liked to consult Roger—but then, if Roger were alive to be consulted, she would not have taken on her fool's errand. "Done," she said.

"Tomorrow?"

They drank another cup on it.

Bradamant awoke to a familiar sensation of knots being tied in her guts. She groaned and pushed herself out from between the sheets. They were not stained, fortunately, so she had only the smallclothes she had worn to bed to throw in the corner for the maidservant to deal with. A pity to make more work, but she could apologize for it later. She hunted about in the pale dawnlight for the soft rags that the steward ought to have provided. She found them at last at the bottom of a chest, some loose and some stitched together along the side. She took one of the tubes, stuffed loose rags inside it, and pinned the ends over her sash to hold the pad in place. She dressed and went down to the kitchens to ask for a tisane. The cook clucked sympathetically and recommended sage and rosemary. It was not much of a breakfast, but the sweet, heavy smell cleared her head, and the hot liquid eased her belly. She wondered if her brother was fox enough to have known.

By sunrise she was at the stable. Renald was already there, saddling Bayard. The bay nuzzled his shoulder. The grey he had ridden home, looked up at the activities beginning, and down again, apparently glad not to be called on for any further use just then. It was cold, and Renald jingled in his mail.

Bradamant hurried to get Marron ready.

They trotted downhill to the same field they had used the day before. This time their shields were clean and fresh-painted, Bradamant's silver with a silver hand on a red cedar, and her brother's red with a silver pile pointing up from the base. A few of the servants, with their cloaks wrapped close around them, followed them out. They were to help in case of injury. Even with the iron lancehead left off, a wooden stave with the weight of a fast horse behind it could do considerable damage.

They could not ride crossways, as they had done before, because of the rising sun, but at the foot of the hill there was a good stretch of level ground beside the road, so that they could ride against each other, and neither one would have the disadvantage of riding into the light or up the slope. Bayard and Marron, both well used to the exercise, took their positions with hardly a touch from either rider.

The gold helm glittered red in the early sunlight.

When they had finished moving into position and halted, Bradamant could hear the birds in the trees nearby celebrating spring and sunrise. A lark, too high to see, was singing in the sky.

Humphrey, with a look of disapproval, shouted, "Let them go!" and dropped his arms.

On the first pass, both struck, but each near the edge of the other's shield. Both turned, letting the blow slip by. They galloped to the ends of the field and wheeled the horses round. Their track was marked with mashed anemones and some scattered divots.

Renald had caught the rhythm, and knew whether he would be at the top, bottom, or center of the horse's stride when his spear touched. The stave crashed into the center of her shield. She fell back, but kept her feet in the stirrups, and was pushed flat on Marron's croup without being shoved off.

Marron staggered and neighed his distress. The force of the blow and the force of Bradamant's own lance changing direction to point at the sky almost toppled him, but he danced, found his balance, and sped on.

Bradamant pulled herself up on the saddlebow and patted Marron. At the touch of the sweaty mane, she felt the rhythm of the step go into her pulse. She turned again.

Renald was aiming for her helmet. If it landed, she would be stunned and thrown. If she ducked, her own stroke would miss. If she raised her shield, she couldn't see. She didn't need to.

Renald's lance skidded up her shield into air. Hers took him on the right shoulder, where his shield did not cover him. He toppled over sideways and back, and thumped to the ground.

Bradamant turned, and rode back. Humphrey was running to meet them, with the other servants following close behind.

Renald lay jingling on the flowers. He was shaking. She held out her hands to help him up, but he did not take them. He squinted against the light at her. She moved round to the shady side and knelt by him. "What is it?"

He put up his hands and fumbled for the helmet, but could not work the strap.

Humphrey reached them and helped him pull the helmet off, thrusting it impatiently at Bradamant to take so that his hands were free to help Renald sit up. Renald paid no attention to where it had gone.

"Bring the cart over," Humphrey told one of the others, then scowled at Bradamant's confusion. "Don't be simple, madame. It's the ague. What would you expect?"

She swallowed to clear her throat. "Will he be all right?"

"Of course," said Renald faintly. "Rest and proper feeding."

Bradamant looked doubtfully at her brother, wondering how much to trust the cure he envisioned. He should not have fought. "Isn't this an excess of gallantry? You must have known, and if you wanted to let me—"

"I didn't want to," he said. "The bad days of a tertian ague should be every third day, and I thought I'd be weak tomorrow. But sometimes it comes early, or maybe I mis-counted the days."

The cart was beside them. Bradamant helped lift Renald up and tucked a blanket around him.

He grinned at her expression. "You could make amends by giving it back," he suggested.

"Well—no."

He nodded and closed his eyes. The cart lurched forward, with Humphrey walking beside it.

Bradamant rode ahead of it to warn the cook that her skill in physicking would be needed again, and to rest a little. Ridding herself of the golden helmet could wait until she felt more like a human.

There were caves and sink-holes in many spots along the course of the Garonne. Opinion divided as to which of these were the work of the river, dropping north out of the Pyrenees, and which had been dug by giants before the Flood.

Bradamant and her brothers had no doubt about the cave nearest Montalban. It was screened by the vines and weeds that grew along the banks of the river, and inside a curving tunnel led to the darkness of a round stone room, where the walls were covered with wild-oxen and hairy elephants. There were still wild-oxen to be found, and the king had a white elephant, the gift of the righteous Saracen, Haroun al Raschid, but she had never heard of a country where hairy elephants ranged.

She went in with a pine torch, and wandered down the cool, mud-smelling passage. The animals, seen in the flickering light, nodded a welcome to her. "Oberon?" she said.

A shadow wavered between two elephants, steadied, and stepped into the light.

Bradamant took the helmet of Mambrino from her head, and put it into Oberon's hands.

He looked up at her. "Do you regret it?"

"Yes."

He tossed it and caught it, balanced spinning on the end of one finger. The gold was bright in the torchlight.

The color faded, growing lighter, with more yellow and less red. The spinning stopped, and Oberon held a basin with a wide brim most of the way round it, such as a barber might use.

"That's brass!"

Oberon nodded and spun it again. It stopped and was gold.

"What is it really?" said Bradamant.

He spun it. "It is what you have eyes to see."

"I can't see it like that," she pointed out.

He blew on it, and it spun faster. "Shall I let you off your word Bradamant? —but we will have use for it in time to come, if you will let it go."

She said nothing.

The yellow brightness gave back the torchlight, seeming as it were itself a light. The light grew smaller, and went out, taking Oberon with it.

An elk on the wall behind him looked for a moment like a horse and skinny rider, but the torch burned higher, and she could see the painted elk tossing its horns against some enemy dead before the Flood.

She had consented, and the golden helmet of Mambrino was gone out of the world.

Chapter 2
The Spear of Galafrone

The sky over Paris was grey, and the grass and the poppies in the fields around seemed to glow of themselves in the even light. The air was damp, misting the heavy cloak Bradamant wore without penetrating the wool.

When she came over the crest of St. Genevieve's hill, the town was spread out beneath her, a tangle of houses and shops coming up the hill from the inside of the bend of the river, under the ward of St. Genevieve's golden church. Its wide dome was not golden at the moment. The bronze gilding was earthcolor under the greys of the shifting clouds.

In the center of the valley, the island of the City floated on the river like a ship ready to follow the current to the sea, towing after it like rafts the pair of marshy islets behind it. On the far side, yet more buildings scrambled up the hill of Martyrs. The city was growing up and out, always cramped, it seemed, no matter how often they abandoned the old walls and built them new, circling more ground.

A string of barges was tied up on the right side of the island. Even though the barges in front were hidden from her by the island itself, she could see from the way the rest floated on the water that they had been unloaded already. There were no workers on the docks. To the palace, then.

She rode down the hill and clopped over the wooden bridge. At the gate she dismounted and leaned back to let the guard in the tower get a look at her.

He waved her in.

The palace was quieter now than it had been in Count Roland's life. But Alda, his widow, was presiding there, and Bradamant could hope to find news of travelers.

Alda was not in the great hall but in her chambers. Isaac, the king's councillor in Jewish matters, was with her, showing off silks from Damascus, and asking her advice on which ladies might be likely to favor which patterns. Bradamant recognized this as a devious way of trying to get Alda to find that she might again have the heart to care about color, and such small matters, herself. Having realized that much, Bradamant realized further that she could not decide if she would be pleased or insulted if Isaac set in on her. Isaac, watching her over a roll of green damasked with griffins, seemed to be turning the same question over in his mind.

Alda ended this dilemma by jumping up to embrace Bradamant and demanding to know her news, and if she had messages from the king, and what brought her to Paris.

"Looking for Marfisa. Any word of her?"

Alda shook her head, but Isaac said, "Lady Marfisa's in Rouen—or she was the other day, when I brought these goods up."

"Why? Is there trouble there?" said Alda.

"No. Some at sea. They wanted a warrior to send out on guard, but it's two days yet till Captain Guichard is supposed to sail."

"The men from the North," said Alda thoughtfully.

"No. Guichard would have complained to you and asked for help. He doesn't know what it is, or he thinks it isn't really anything, or he thinks it's something unchancy. I don't know which. He can keep his own counsel, Guichard."

"You traders do," said Alda. "But I'd like to know what's what, all the same. Tell him to send me word."

Bradamant scrambled after Isaac into a barge, feeling awkwardly about for clear spaces to put her feet. The two boatmen, checking off their tally of goods, looked up to nod a greeting, and gave their names as Arnold and Jacques. It was mizzling again, and behind the clouds the sun was not up yet. The boatmen were leaving early to avoid rowing against the bore of the tide when they came near the mouth of the river. It was a pity to leave Marron behind in a Paris stable, but the river was easier and smoother than the road to Rouen, and Marron could do with a rest.

Isaac had no goods going downriver—he was going to bring another load of fabrics and metalwork up—but the barge was crammed with outgoing traffic from other dealers: wines, wool cloth, early vegetables, all the produce for trade in the northwest, funnelled along the Oise, the Marne, and the Yonne to the Seine.

Once in Rouen, the goods would spread out again, to the villages around, and to the ships in the harbor.

Isaac tapped Bradamant's shoulder and pointed at the extra oars stowed at the sides, glowered at the river, and, for good measure, at the sky. He pulled his hood closer on his ears. A terrier bitch sitting on the front edge of the boat leaped up enthusiastically, came running to sniff at Isaac, considered Bradamant, and made ready to yap.

"That's a friend, Preacher," said Arnold.

Preacher sniffed some more to memorize Bradamant and strutted to her place at the front again to supervise.

Bradamant and Isaac found more or less clear spots between bales, near the extra oars, and wriggled in.

The boatmen finished their check and pushed off into the current.

At first the land on either side of them was as colorless as the sky and the river, lines of grey on fields of grey marking off one from the other. Then gradually, as the invisible sun went up the sky, the fields took on their colors—the different greens of new grass, wheat, or oats, blue bellflowers, yellow dandelions.

In the afternoon, they came to the marshes near Rouen. Spikes of purple loosestrife stood tall wherever the water was shallow.

The rowing went more slowly, to keep clear of rocks and hidden banks of mud. When they ran into mud anyway, they poled off and tried a new slant. As they lurched free of one such bank, Preacher jumped to her feet, and set to barking her head off.

The boatmen gave one frantic push, putting them afloat again, while Bradamant and Isaac each grabbed for a spare oar, ready to strike out.

Then the gargoyles that infested the swamps were upon them, swarming up over the sides of the boat, snapping with their flint-like teeth at anything they could swallow—wine, wheat, plates, people, wool, vegetables, glassware—whether it was edible or not. There were those who said it didn't matter, as gargoyles could digest anything. Others said it didn't matter, as gargoyles could excrete anything.

The creatures' hides were too thick and tough to cut with a sword—unless it was magic—but they did not like to be clubbed and yelled at. Preacher, who knew her business, did not try to bite even the ones as small as herself, but ran barking up and down, producing a noise that seemed much too large to have been inside her.

After a long few minutes, a gargoyle with wings screamed and launched itself away from them, flapping wildly to get out of range of the oars and the noise. Its wings were not big enough to carry it far, but as it hit the water it set about pumping its arms and legs, and half-swam, half-flew over the mud flats. It fled complaining, kicking down the loosestrife in its way, and first one, then another, then the whole pack followed screeching after.

Jacques caught up Preacher and set about calming her. The others sat down, to check damages.

Isaac had a torn sleeve and under it a long scratch. Bradamant had a bruised foot, but the gargoyle had not had time to bite through the leather of her boot. Arnold was bleeding from a bite in the leg. He pulled out a roll of clean rags from under his seat. Bradamant took them and started to dip one in the water, but hesitated, seeing how muddy it was. Arnold shook his head and pointed to a pot of mineral water.

Jacques let go of the dog and joined Bradamant in cleaning and binding up the wound, finishing in time to fend them off from another mud-bank. The water was still shallow, and he poled them slowly downriver, following the sluggish current.

Arnold took hold of the seat, to steady himself against the stops and starts the mud and poling gave their course. He looked down at his leg. "Good pair of leggings, too."

"A lesson against vanity," said Jacques.

"You're a great comfort, you are. Let's have a drop."

Jacques handed him a jug of wine.

Meanwhile, Isaac had pulled off his tunic and cleaned his arm. Then he took a needle and thread from his pouch, as his dignity could not suffer arriving in Rouen with torn clothes. "They're bad this year," he said, biting off a length of thread. He was getting too old to catch the needle's eye with any ease. Jacques, who had the advantage of a little nearsightedness, as well as younger eyes, threaded the needle for him, and Isaac set about his repairs.

"Well—" said Arnold, glancing mournfully at his bitten leg "—bad this time. Cuts into the profits, too. But not bad this year, no." He and Preacher both yelped as the boat jarred against a stone.

"Sorry," said Jacques.

Bradamant leaned out to push them away from the stone. It was the shape of a gargoyle.

"No," said Arnold again, "Not to say bad. There's a spell been put on them, or a spell wore off, or something, and they're not so many as they were. Time's coming the problem's going to be getting those carcasses out of the river. They don't seem to rot proper, no more than a real stone would."

"Not our problem," said Jacques. "Plenty enough of them still alive. You'd better eat something, too."

At Rouen the river opened out, wider and deeper, large enough for ships to come directly in from the sea. The land was marshy on both sides, but the advantages of controlling the sea-trade had been obvious for centuries. The Rotomagians had managed to tamp enough layers of earth and rock under their foundations to keep their feet dry.

Some traders' prentices showed up on the dock when they arrived, ostensibly to help them unload, but really more for the excitement of helping Arnold out and hearing the story of the battle.

Isaac went in search of his local trade-partner, and Bradamant pulled one of the youngsters out of the pack to give her a shoulder and take her to Guichard's house. Although her foot did not actually hurt much, she made the most of the limp to make the story better.

Her sister-in-law was sitting in front at Guichard's, brushing her mail and digging bits of dirt out. She had polished her shield already. The gold phoenix and border gleamed against the green field. The dragon on her helmet was still dull, waiting attention.

"Hey."

Marfisa dropped the mailshirt, which fell ringing to the ground, and jumped up to hug her. Bradamant bent down to the embrace, for Marfisa was only of middle height.

Marfisa held up a finger in token of "one moment" and dodged into the house, from which she returned with a mug of cider in each hand and, on her fingertips, poised precariously between the mugs, a bowl of soft blue cheese with some crackers heaped on top. "There'll be tripe stew for supper," she reported, "but you look as if a bite now would do."

Bradamant sat down on the bench, took a mug, scooped up cheese on a cracker, and looked at the mailshirt. "What you need," she said, "is a barrel of sand."

Marfisa humphed. "No point to getting off rust *before* you go to sea. I just need to look presentable, more or less. But what, O my sister, brings you to Rouen?"

"You."

"How did you know I was— Oh. Master Isaac?"

Bradamant nodded, and plunged into the question. "Will you let me have Galafrone's spear back?"

"Of course."

Bradamant started to relax.

"—when I'm done with it," she added cheerfully.

Bradamant gave her a sideways glance. "And when's that?"

"This voyage, with luck. What's the need?" Marfisa gave up the mailshirt and went after her helmet.

Bradamant told of her meeting with Oberon and the quest he had asked her to undertake, of returning fairy gifts.

Marfisa heard her out in silence, and was silent a moment longer, thinking it over. "And you feel sure he was a good genie, not an evil one?" she said at last.

"Partly that. But he's right that these things don't belong to our world, and if they want them back it seems only right to let them have them."

"What if they want them to use against us?"

Bradamant thought about it. "If they wanted to do harm to mortals, they have craftier ways. I've never heard that they mounted battle against us—why would they change now?"

"For amusement," Marfisa suggested.

"That would be stupid."

"Can't they be stupid?"

"I don't think Oberon is."

Marfisa grunted, conceding the point, but went on, "And why you? Let them run their own errands! You have better things to do."

"What?"

"What's wrong with guarding traders?" Marfisa grinned suddenly and added, "Can be interesting."

"Is it usually?"

Marfisa took the last of the cheese. "Sometimes." She pointed a finger at her sister-in-law and said, over the cheese, "Come with me this trip. I need some bait."

The tide, for a wonder, let the warriors sleep late, although Guichard and his household were up early to complete the loading of the *Ramsbottom* and to check last-minute fittings. Bradamant and Marfisa turned over on their pallet and stuffed their heads under the pillows to avoid waking up completely before they had to.

The *Ramsbottom* had a crew of near 30, enough to row, if the wind failed them, but it was built for wind, a large, three-masted ship, tireless as the lamb of Rouen, which stood with one hoof up, always ready for another step.

The sails had not been unfurled on the yards, but the masts were already bright with canvas flags—the lamb of Rouen, a sea-blue ramping ram for Guichard, Marfisa's gold phoenix on its green oasis, and Bradamant's silver hand and red cedar.

With Guichard and one of his mates, the two women rowed the longboat to the ship, and boarded.

Guichard whistled for attention, and the crew gathered around them. He jerked a thumb up at the sky. "What do you say to the wind and the weather?" he asked.

"Leave on the tide?" said one.

He nodded.

The men looked at each other, and the water, and the sky. "Aye, sir," came the answer, except for one snub-nosed, short-bearded man who looked to the east, stiffened his back and his expression, and said, "Captain, I have my doubts about the weather."

There was a groan from the rest.

"I note your advice," said Guichard, "but the crew consents. Do you want to be put ashore?"

"No, Captain."

Guichard nodded and turned away. "Up anchor!" he said, and pointed off three men to the capstan, with two more to go up the webs of the main mast and set its sail as soon as the *Ramsbottom* was free.

When they cleared the river and entered ocean, the other two sails were lowered, and lashed down on the deck. With its full canvas now set, the ship sped forward, shaking in the waves of the Channel.

The sailor who had objected to the weather went to the rail to throw up.

"Does he always?" said Marfisa.

"Always," said Guichard. "But then he's good at stowing cargo and figuring profits. And how are *you?*" He looked at both passengers carefully.

"Me?" said Marfisa. "It's about like riding a camel. I'm fine."

Bradamant added quickly, so as not to give herself time to think more about it, "I'm well enough, but give me something to do."

Guichard turned, scanning the deck. "You could help with the forecastle, Lady."

She hurried to the prow and joined the sailors who, under the mate's direction, were setting up the little fortress of wood and leather that protected the guard there in time of attack. When that chore was finished, she looked for Marfisa, and saw her at the stern, leaning over to watch the dark waves and the gulls following the ship. Behind them, a flock of sandpipers, already as small as dots on the shoreline, screamed with delight as they hunted for cockles in the mud.

Bradamant made her way cautiously over the deck. Her legs were beginning to remember how to give way to the roll of the ship, so that she could walk without staggering.

"Forecastle's ready," she told Marfisa.

"Don't need it yet," said Marfisa ungratefully. "Wouldn't be any point to attacking us in sight of land."

"All the same—"

"And there's a lookout in the crow's nest, anyway."

"So it'll be a while before you drop me."

"Yes. Why don't you sit down and enjoy—" Marfisa reconsidered. "Would you like to check the battleground?"

"Yes."

They went below deck into the hold. It was too dark to see much at first. Bradamant stopped halfway down the gangplank, waiting to see what footing she would find, and sniffed at the smells below.

The hold was almost dry, she realized. Although a little saltwater sloshed noisily over the line of the keel, it was new water. Instead of mildew and bilgewater, there were only the smells of the spices in the cargo: green ginger, ginger cured in lemon juice, cinnamon, and pepper. Chests marked with the seals of their merchants hid away loads of dried fruits, rare woods, fine woolen cloths from Rouen and Paris, velvets from Tours and linens from as far south as Lyons.

"Lady?" said a voice from the back of the hold.

"No signs?" Marfisa asked.

"No, Lady." A chest creaked as the sailor sat down again.

"You aren't going to fall asleep down here?" said Marfisa.

"No chance, Lady," said a second voice. A small rattling sound followed.

The two sailors bent over the chest between them, squinting. Only a little light came through cracks into the hold.

"You lose," said the first.

"I swear those are weighted," said the second.

"Don't blame me—it's your set."

"How much can they do if something breaks through down here?" said Bradamant.

"Well, some little help. Depends how big a hole it makes and how quickly our boys here spot it. They yell for me to come down and fight it, and meanwhile everyone else gets down here fast and bails like mad. Or else we give it up as a bad job and try to get away in the boats. A pair down here is just as well. But the hold watch is a measure in reserve. What we want is an attack we can see."

"Bait," said Bradamant.

"Bait," Marfisa agreed.

There was a snorting noise from both the sailors, either in protest at the whole plan or at the dice.

Bradamant and Marfisa went up the gangway and crawled out on deck. They sat there blinking until their eyes were used to the light again. Bradamant gulped at the horizon rising and falling. She had been so absorbed in their check of the guards that she had managed not to notice her discomfort, but the view brought it back. "Why don't you drop me now?" she suggested. "No harm in caution."

"No sea-legs yet?" said Marfisa sympathetically.

"No."

Lowering the boat was a procedure that involved yet more swaying, and a little bumping against the *Ramsbottom's* side as well, but once the boat was in the water and took its own level, Bradamant began to feel better. It was too short to straddle more than one wave at a time, and so, although it pitched up and down, it neither rolled nor yawed.

On board the *Ramsbottom*, Marfisa and two of the sailors hauled the rope forward, until Bradamant's boat floated near the prow, warded from above by the forecastle.

Bradamant ate some bread and hard cheese, prayed for the success of their fishing, and then for friends and kinfolk. She lost herself in memories of them.

When the attack came, it was too sudden for her to call out a warning.

The boat rose out of the water and spilled over as she grabbed hold of the gunwale. The water was cold. She felt heavy. If she let go, her mail would drag her down before she could get out of it.

She let go with one hand, and used the hand she had freed to draw her sword. The weight felt wrong, pulling the blade through water. Then it felt right. The buoyancy of the wood had dragged her up into air. She gasped for breath.

The sea-orc, whistling shrilly, rose out of the water, a long, white line, rising into a curve that led down again to the bait. Its great jaws closed on Bradamant and plucked her away from her hold on the boat.

She huddled into a ball.

Its teeth were sharp, but not flint. It could not chew through her mail. It screamed out another whistle, swept its tail up, and brought it crashing down, staving in one side of the boat.

She could not get room to cut at it, but she stabbed at it down its throat.

It screamed and spat her out. Raising its tail again, it struck heavily at the side of the ship.

Yells came from inside.

Bradamant flailed her arms and legs wildly. She found the capsized boat and caught hold of it before the weight of her mail could pull her under. Kicking out to help shove herself against the drag of the water, she pulled herself back along the boat, trying to move away from the space between the ship and the sea-orc, to give Marfisa a clear target.

The spear of Galafrone gleamed in the air, falling out of the blue sky, and sizzled over Bradamant's shoulder. True to its magic, it landed square in the sea-orc's body, biting deep into its neck.

The sea-orc screamed again and struck at the ship again. The planks screamed back, ripping free from each other. A breach had opened.

Bradamant grabbed hold of the rope attached to the spear, pulled herself closer, and grabbed the spear itself. It was something to hang on to—and she thought the extra pain of the drag on its wound might discourage the sea-orc from smashing in the ship any further.

Apparently, it did.

The sea-orc raced away over the waters, rippling its long length from side to side and building speed.

From the forecastle above, Marfisa let out rope, playing the sea-orc like a fish.

Bradamant thought it would try to lunge forward and break the rope when it came to the end and found itself held. Instead, it lunged back toward the ship and caught the rope in its teeth before Marfisa could haul in the slack. The rope gave way, and the sea-orc rocked, free in the waves. It screeched and fled to the north, heedless of the extra weight clinging at its side.

Bradamant inched one hand along the spear and caught hold again of the remnant of rope still fastened to it. She lashed herself to the spear, close in to the sea-orc's body, so that her head was supported against it, and she would still be able to go on breathing when the water chilled her into sleep—that is, if she didn't choke on the spume blowing against her in the meantime, and if the sea-orc didn't decide to swim underwater. It seemed to make better speed on the surface, and she hoped for the best.

The sky was blue, and the water was blue. The foam was white, and the sea-orc's coat of fur was white. She tried calling out to Oberon, but the middle of the Channel was apparently not a place of power to him.

She grew colder.

Singing woke her, voices lamenting. They called to one another, weeping melodies.

Bradamant tried to open her eyes, but it was hard to make the effort.

Then something beside her, its voice surging in her head, like an earthquake rather than a noise, answered the singers. So close, she could not make out the tone, but only the steady, lapping rhythm of it.

The sea-orc was singing back.

She got her eyes open. She was still in the water, and too numb to feel the cold. The sea-orc was not making much speed. It was swimming feebly.

A flock of white-furred...seals?...was plunging at them over the waves, from the rocky shore beyond.

No, not seals. They had long tails, not flippers. They had hands and arms, and bright green eyes. They had manes of long white hair on their heads, and some had babies clinging to their hair. Most of those so occupied had curving breasts, but the others were flat. A thin vertical line coming down just below their bellies marked their privates.

One, slower than the rest, still behind on shore, finished running a comb through the mane of hair. The gold of the comb glittered. Then even that one was in the water and racing to help the sea-orc.

The northern mermaids pressed close around the sea-orc, cooing at it and half-supporting it. Two of them inspected Bradamant, converging on the spear, where it thrust into the orc. They sang to each other in a language Bradamant did not understand. They sounded angry and sorrowful. Bradamant tried to draw her sword, but her hand was too cold to find it by touch. She looked down, trying to close her fingers on it.

But the mermaids paid her no heed. They scowled, and made what sounded like threats for later, but their first concern was for the orc. Each took a little jar of ointment from the pouch about her waist, and some half dozen more came near, with pads of seaweed in their hands. Then the first two seized the spear and pulled it, with Bradamant, away from the wound.

The sea-orc bellowed and thrashed. Its attendants closed in, singing and sighing. First the ointment was applied, and then the seaweed bandage, pressed close by mermaids singing songs of healing. Others were twisting a rope of seaweed, to bind the pads in place.

Bradamant, with the weight of her armor and the spear, sank beneath the water. She tried to call "Oberon," but it came out "Glub." She began fumbling with the rope to free herself from the spear. Trusting in desperation to the spear's magic, when she had it loose she threw it up with one hand, towards the shore, and caught hold of the rope-end with the other hand.

The spear embedded itself in sand, between rocks, just where a wave was falling on the shore.

Bradamant fell clangorously on the stony beach, and was pushed to the ground by another wave, crashing ashore in its turn. She swallowed salt-water, but the force of the wave pushed her over the stones, out of the reach of the waves following behind.

She threw up, and lay with her cheek on a round, black stone, coughing and gasping for air.

When she caught her breath and sat up, she found herself watched. Beside her stood Oberon, dressed in black and gold, and holding the magic spear. Facing her, bobbing up and down as the waves came in, and balanced on the curve of her tail, was one of the mermaids, white fur gleaming silver in the sunlight.

The mermaid scowled from one to the other, fixed her frown on Bradamant for a long moment, then said to Oberon. "Is that yours?"

"You may say so."

"I am the liege of King Charlemagne!" Bradamant protested.

Oberon held up one hand to shush her.

The mermaid broke in, "Listen, ship-rider, and make your people hear! The seas are ours. Trees belong on the land, and so do you. We will destroy all of you who enter our realm. Tell your people!"

Oberon nodded at the injured sea-orc. "You mean you will kill some. How many of you have the will to die for it?"

"All," she replied.

He shrugged. "Well, if you all mean that, we'll miss you. But there are oceans beyond these—and they're drawing farther apart. If you linger too long fighting for the honor of these, you'll lose the way home." He knelt to her. "Come home. We would miss you."

"You would miss the music."

"That, too," he agreed. He looked out over the waves. The mermaids were coaxing the sea-orc down under. "You could use the spear, I think. A rune for healing a wound works better with the weapon responsible."

The mermaid hesitated.

He rubbed first one knee and then the other, where stones were poking him, and said, "Shall I beg, or stand?"

"Swim," she said, and flung herself into the wave and was gone.

Oberon climbed to his feet, pulling himself up on the spear. He rubbed his legs and winked at Bradamant. "Don't carry the merfolks' challenge," he said. He jumped into the water and slid away on the undertow, spear in hand. He shot through the water as if he was flying rather than swimming in it. The spear opened up a furrow in the water, a long silver gleam vanishing behind as quickly as it opened ahead.

Bradamant pulled off her armor and clothes, spread them to dry, and found a sunny hollow to crouch in, out of the wind. One of the stones was large and smooth enough to provide tolerable sitting.

She managed to doze off, and when she woke her things were dry, or pretty nearly.

Shivering, she climbed into them. She felt stiff, and her stomach was starting to rumble.

She wondered where Marfisa was, and the ship. Marfisa would be amused if she knew how they had succeeded in disposing of the monster that threatened the shipping. At least, it looked like a success. Oberon seemed to have no doubts.

And the magic spear of Galafrone was now lost to mortal hands. She was a little sorry. She took pride in using her own skill in a human joust, but there was nothing like magic for fighting a monster.

She stared at the cliffs that edged the shingle, looking for a way up. She must be somewhere on the English coast. If she went inland, she would come to human homes.

Chapter 3
Astolf's Book

When she came to Astolf's castle, Bradamant's necklace of gold and silver links was shorter than it had been, and her feet were sore.

Astolf was outside the oak walls, in a clover meadow, sprinkling sand on a swarm of bees, and chanting a rune to make them choose a place nearby for the new hive—preferably, the box he had already set for them.

"Settle, women of victory, sink to the ground," he said. "Never fly wild to the wood."

The clover smell and the buzz and the rune made her sway, drowsily. She was tempted to sit down in the grass, but suspected she would have trouble getting up again. As he finished and turned slowly away, Bradamant said, "I'd think they'd sting."

"I'm not afraid, so they don't. Swarming bee has better things to think about anyway." But he moved slowly until he was well away from the swarm. Then he embraced Bradamant heartily, saying, "Come in, rest, tell all the news." He looked at her quickly. "The king well?"

"Yes."

Astolf gave her his arm, seeing her limp, and brought her through the palisade-gate, under his banner. It was blue, with a gold saltire in token of the kingdom of Mercia, between two gold leopards. A row of silver circles ran round the edge. His face had a few more lines about the eyes, but his mustache and beard hid any lines at the mouth. His straight brown hair was lightened by lines of grey, with a bald spot at the back of his head. He was not as skinny as he used to be.

They entered the great hall. Like the palisade, it was built of strong oak from the forests around Lichfield.

Lady Sylvia looked up from going over a tally of the rising crops with the steward Wilfrid. She rose to her full height, taller than her son, almost as tall as Bradamant. The bronze key ornament hanging from her belt, marking her status as lady of the manor, clicked against her knees as she sailed forward to welcome her niece.

In moments, Bradamant was sitting on a cushioned bench against the wall, so that she could lean back, with bread and honey in front of her, and cheese, and a silver horn of mulberry wine to drink.

Bradamant did not feel like explaining her errand immediately. It was a long story, and now that she was sitting down she was tired. And it would be easier to tell Astolf alone, who had fought beside her, than to tell her formidable aunt. Instead, she offered Lady Sylvia her condolence on the death of Sylvia's husband, and received condolence on the death of her own. "When I landed, I thought I might hear that Astolf had been chosen High King," Bradamant remarked.

"Not for me," said Astolf. "Let Cenwulf have Mercia—and try for the rest, if he likes."

Lady Sylvia considered him, and glanced around the hall to see who was in earshot, and said, "Cenwulf's a poor choice. Bishop Alcuin's been complaining to Charlemagne already that the new kings in Northumbria and Mercia don't come of the old stock."

"They do if you go back far enough," said Astolf.

"Your fifth cousin, or so, if you believe that," Sylvia returned.

"Royal enough. And he's an able ruler, so far."

Lady Sylvia tapped at her keys. "You must not do yourself injustice. You would do well as the Bretwalda." She added to Bradamant, "But don't say I think so."

"I'm sorry," Bradamant said. "I shouldn't have spoken of it."

"Only us. No harm," said Astolf. He took a sip of mulberry and said thoughtfully, "Might not be best for my health to speak of other places. Like Wessex."

Lady Sylvia smoothed the bronze key-hanger on her lap, and gave a nod of agreement. The bretwalda—the one who could wield Britain—might not have direct power over other kingdoms, but he could do much to make life easier or harder for the whole of the island. Egbert of Wessex hoped to gain control of the West Saxons and the overlordship of the seven kingdoms. A quarrel among the Mercian nobles could be of use to him.

Wilfrid came back and said there was a bower made ready for Lady Bradamant in one of the little cabins outside the main hall.

"Would you like Astolf to show you the way?"

It would be easier to tell Astolf alone—but perhaps not the wisest thing either to ask him to keep a secret from Lady Sylvia or to have him tell her. Lady Sylvia would wonder why she could not speak for herself.

"I wanted to ask your advice," she said, looking at both of them.

The steward bowed and went away to his tally records again, rubbing at a smudge of ink on one thumb.

Astolf rested his chin on his hands. Lady Sylvia waited without stirring.

Bradamant ordered her thoughts and explained the quest Oberon had set her. "Marfisa wondered if he might have lied to me, but he didn't seem to me like someone who would," she ended, in case either of them meant to offer the same suggestion.

"Story sounds likely enough," Astolf commented. "Magic's drawing further off—harder to command."

"That might be as well," said his mother.

Astolf shook his head, but did not argue the point. "Your cousin Malgis would have noticed it, too," he said, with a questioning look. He was too courteous to ask directly what his fellow magician had made of this project of hers.

"He goes away winters—wasn't back in the Ardennes yet when I crossed it," she explained.

A quirky smile showed on his face for a moment. He did not seem to think Malgis would think much of it.

"Will you help me?" Bradamant said anyway.

"What do you want?" said Astolf, warily.

"The hippogriff and—"

"You're joking!"

"No, of course not."

"Would you give away Marron? Renald give away Bayard? Hippogriff's my friend."

"Try asking the hippogriff," said Lady Sylvia.

Astolf hesitated, pulling at his beard. "If you really want to give things back to the good neighbors, you don't want to give them hippogriff, anyway."

"Why not?"

"Can't get at other things, some of them—not without wings. Bargain?"

"What's the bargain?"

"Take hippogriff while you search. But give him back to me. He isn't magic."

"Not magic? Born of a griffin and a mare?"

"They breed them in the Riphaean mountains," he said.

"A difficult mating, I should think," commented Lady Sylvia.

Bradamant, too, had heard that the hippogriff was a sort of mule. First you get an eagle to tread a lioness. (Or you get a lion to mount an eagle, which sounded even harder to arrange.) That gives you a griffin, and by then you should have the skills to get a griffin to mount a mare, or to get a griffin mounted by a stallion, without damage to the horse. Or the griffin. Or yourself. Not magic. Not magic? Well, that was the story.

"I agree to bring the hippogriff back," she said. "But I'll ask you for him again."

Astolf gave a little sigh. "You can ask," he said.

Lady Sylvia clicked her tongue, but all she said was, "*and*?"

"Oh!" said Bradamant. "—And the magic horn and book the fairy Logistilla gave you."

"Welcome to the horn," said Astolf. "It lost its voice in the air somewhere on the way back from the Moon. I thought—"

Lady Sylvia smiled at him.

Ruefully, he smiled back, and explained to Bradamant, "Mother thinks my thought was the same—well, have to admit, it was. You say the good neighbors think we shouldn't have it. And probably right: Just as well not to have it. Horn's power was to terrify all who heard it. Wasn't good for anything else. Thought it might be dangerous with its voice back, might get into the wrong hands." He looked down at his own, and up at Bradamant. "Didn't try to find the voice."

"And the book?"

"Oh, the book! Don't have it."

"Who does?" said Bradamant patiently.

"Cenwulf. Hostage for my good behavior."

She goggled at him. "Isn't *that* dangerous in the wrong hands?"

"Not much. Its power is breaking spells, mostly. And he doesn't have anyone who can open it."

Bradamant mused. "Will he fight if I challenge him?"

"Not if he has half the wits he needs," said Lady Sylvia.

"I wouldn't," said Astolf. He traced his finger along a frayed bit of silver thread in the embroidery of his tunic. "Wouldn't be very hard to steal it, except that—" He stopped and grinned suddenly at them both. "Is it stealing? —book's mine."

"It is not stealing," Lady Sylvia replied. "But it would be unfortunate if the king reasoned that you had done it."

"Words right out of my mouth," said Astolf.

"Yes, you'd be the obvious one to suspect," Bradamant said.

"If the good neighbors want it, the good neighbors should take it themselves," Lady Sylvia said, irritably.

"I don't think they can," Bradamant answered.

Astolf sat up. "But you don't know. Most people think they steal—changelings, milk, the foison of a harvest—" He fell silent.

"Come along," said Lady Sylvia after a moment. "I'll show you to the bath-house and your bower. You're tired, I know, and there's no telling how long he'll sit like that, brooding a notion."

At first Bradamant found it difficult to fall asleep. There was a tapestry in the bower, an intricate weaving that showed Prince Brutus of Troy and Prince Woden of Asia weeping over the ruins of the fallen city as they made ready to flee into the West. One eagle-banner still stood, but its end had already burst into flames. Instead of staring at the walls of Troy, as they were supposed to do, the princes seemed to be staring at Bradamant and talking about her. She strained to hear what they said, but she could not make it out. She wondered if it was a wandering bit of Astolf's magic, or if she was already asleep and in a dream.

Astolf took her the following day to the stable with some strips of beef and a handful of oats, to meet the hippogriff. From a corner of the main building one tower rose up, marking a line of shadow across the stable. It gave Astolf a clear view of the stars and planets.

The hippogriff eyed her suspiciously, turning his eagle head from side to side to get a good look at her, and shifting nervously from foot to foot. The hooves in front tapped on the cobblestones, and the paws in back made a shuffling sound, with a click every now and then as a claw touched stone. He sprang out of his stall, trotted to the stable door, and went into a gallop, spreading his long white wings. He rose from the ground. He cleared the palisade and was off into the sky, swerving once to miss the star-tower.

Bradamant looked at Astolf. He held up a hand for them to wait in silence.

In a few minutes the hippogriff stooped and plunged down, cupping his wings as he landed at a run, and furling them as he sped through the door. He pulled up with a screech in front of Astolf and grabbed a strip of beef from him, then held it daintily in place on the ground with one hoof while tearing off bites.

When the strip was gone, Astolf held out some of the oats.

The hippogriff pecked them up.

Astolf said, "This is my friend Bradamant."

Bradamant held out a strip of beef.

The hippogriff accepted it.

While he ate, Astolf explained their plan.

The hippogriff also accepted a few oats.

When Astolf fell silent, the hippogriff eyed them carefully, but without fidgeting. Then he knelt down in front of them.

"Thank you," said Bradamant, first holding out her hand as a signal of her intention to come closer, and then embracing him. The head plumage was soft and downy. She looked wondering at the hippogriff, which returned her gaze, cocking its head from side to side to get a view of her in both eyes. "Do you understand speech?"

The hippogriff snorted.

"Not sure. More than a horse does," said Astolf

"That's more than most people think," said Bradamant.

Astolf nodded solemnly.

A leather collar hid the line at the base of neck and wings where white feathers gave way to coarse, tawny hair.

"Are you magic?"

The hippogriff gave a series of little screeches, in rhythm like a horse-laugh.

* * *

Astolf rode away to London. Cenwulf was holding court there, to honor the king of Essex, and to try to gain support for his scheme of moving the archbishop's seat from Canterbury to London. He already had the support of the other kings in reducing Lichfield to a bishopric, but Wessex, across the river, was not eager to let the sole archbishop of England go to London, under Cenwulf's control.

Bradamant stayed behind a few days, glad of the rest, both to ease her feet and to let her month begin.

Before dawn on the fourth day, Lady Sylvia woke her and said farewell. "Take care of the boy," she said. "He's stubborn."

"Yes, I'll try," said Bradamant. She crept to the stable. It seemed odd to be setting off without armor.

She took the vials Astolf had left for her. One she wrapped in wool and put in her pouch. She drank a gulp of the other. It tasted of mint, but under the flavoring was a thick bitterness. She followed it quickly with a honeydrop, then poured a little more of the potion into a bucket of water. She corked what was left and put it in the pouch, with a few more honeydrops.

The hippogriff sniffed and pecked at her arm.

Bradamant put her hand at the base of his neck to gentle him.

She couldn't see her hand.

She looked down. She couldn't see the rest of her, either.

She offered the bucket to the hippogriff, who consented to drink, although he liked it as little as Bradamant did. He snatched up a few mouthfuls of wheat after it, and vanished while he was still gulping them down.

Bradamant felt for his back and climbed up. She took hold of the grips on the collar, and the hippogriff again ran from the stable and took to the air.

The castle fell away beneath them.

Forest stretched as far as she could see, an ocean of green leaves. The road that led away from the castle and the clearing for the estate grew smaller as they rose. The woods went on beneath them.

The wind made it hard to breathe. The beating of the wings was like a roar, so close to her ears. She put her head close down by the hippogriff's, presenting as little of herself to the rushing air as she could manage. The trees and the line of the road were steady, unchanging, beneath them.

In the afternoon they came to Londontown.

"There," said Bradamant, and the hippogriff circled out of the sky to land beside the river, between Caesar's Tower and London Bridge.

The Conqueror's Tower was fortress, court, feast hall, prison, mint, and treasury. It faced south, dominating the bridge, the entrance through Southwark into the kingdom of Wessex. At the moment, to those inside, the feast hall, on the first floor above ground level, was the most important. Insolent with the strength of walls eight feet thick, the Tower had windows let in on all sides. The hall shutters were open, and the High King's feast could be heard reveling inside—people eating, drinking, talking, laughing, serving. A singer's voice cut through the noise, high and sweet, telling how Prince Woden learned magic when he hung on the tree.

Was that Cenwulf's choice? Bradamant wondered.

Flags were flying from the four turrets, one at each corner of the Tower. Cenwulf had the Mercian saltire, and Astolf his saltire and staring leopards. There were three gold sax-blades on red for the King of Essex, and London's St. Peter, holding two swords, flew from the last turret.

St. Peter's was her turret. The hippogriff flew her once around the battlements, so that she could look through the windows to check that the southeast turret was still the treasury, and that the turret walls were thinner than the main fortress, about two feet thick. The hippogriff could have managed to crawl through the lower windows, but that was not quite what she and Astolf wanted.

The hippogriff soared out across the Thames, circled round over Southwark, and arrowed in—not on the turret window, which was barred, but on the window of the courtroom below, which was only shuttered.

At the last moment, the hippogriff furled his wings and flattened himself out. Bradamant lay stretched out flat along the length of him. The impact of the horse-hooves crashed the shutters open, and they were in, except for the hippogriff's lion-paws, hooked inside the depth of the window. He tried not to screech, and gave an angry choking sound instead.

Bradamant picked herself up off the floor and helped him down, checking to see that he was not hurt. He pulled his paws away when she first tried to touch them, then let her set her hand to the creased fur. Bruises, she thought, but they weren't bad ones.

"Come when I whistle," she said.

He stood up and shook himself vigorously, opening and closing his wings. His feathers rustled as he preened them. Then he nudged her gently out of his way, and she heard him walk inwards a few paces, limping just a little as he stepped on his hind legs. He turned, ran back, and made the leap out, this time without catching so much as a hair. He was gone.

Bradamant made her invisible way into the center of the Tower and found the narrow, spiral staircase that took her up into the turret.

The treasury door was locked and guarded, so her first task was to thump the guard over the head with her fists clenched together.

He went down, clattering on the stone floor. He looked as if he would be all right, but Bradamant had seen many kinds of injuries in King Charlemagne's wars, and she knew that such a blow could do more damage, sometimes, than the look of it suggested. So she hurried on to the next task, which was to pick the lock.

Bradamant had been a mischievous little girl, with mischievous brothers to egg her on. When she was ten, she was fairly good at picking locks. But when she began training in the use of knightly weapons, she was not given much time for other things, especially mischief, and her hands shook as she began. How did it go? And how did it go with invisible pins? She was clumsy, dropping the pins, which came into view as they fell, or getting them caught in the stiff lock. Then her hands remembered the old skill and stopped shaking.

The door swung open.

Bradamant spotted the great book and rushed to it, ignoring the ordinary gold and jewels and dies for minting coins in the chamber. The book was chained to the floor, but she picked that lock, too. She traced the pattern which Astolf had shown her on the cover. She wondered what the binding was—it felt sturdy like leather, but shone like silk. She could not tell what it was. It seemed as if it glimmered with all colors, a sheer fabric shot through with rainbows, and then it seemed as if it was deep and grey, drifting like rain-clouds. She turned her head aside, so as not to look at it too long. The pages sighed like a whisper and came loose. She opened the book to the table of contents, then turned to the index, where she found the spells to heal injury and restore the lack of substance.

She wondered if the fairies were really so carefully organized among themselves, or if Logistilla had done it that way for mortal convenience.

With the book safely open, she brought out the vial wrapped in wool. The potion to turn herself visible was easier to swallow than its counterpart. It was tart, like rose-hips, and puckered her mouth, but there was no bitterness to it.

When she had swallowed a gulp, she turned the book to the spell against injury. She knelt by the unconscious guard, put her hand on his head, and read the spell aloud. She did not understand the words, but as she spoke them she felt herself growing warm and sleepy, as if she had been wrapped in something soft. There was a lavender smell.

The guard moaned, and then gave a snore.

Bradamant left him in the hallway to wake up by himself and went to the window. Consulting the book's index again, she found the spell to heal lack of substance. She set her arm against the iron bars and read it backward, taking the words in reverse. This time it made her feel cold and windy. The sleepiness was the same, though. She yawned, swallowed hard, and forced her eyes open, concentrating on the page.

But the bars still felt hard against her arms. She looked at them, feeling a touch of panic somewhere inside her. Astolf had said it was hard to use the book to cast spells, and getting harder. Perhaps she ought to have read the spell backward by sounding the letters of the words backwards.

She tried that. It made her feel colder and sleepier.

The guard was not awake, but someone from below must have heard something. There were footsteps coming up the stairwell.

The iron bars were cold against her arms.

She heard wings outside the window, and something she could not see screeched.

She got out of the way just in time as it swooped in through the barred window.

"I didn't whistle," she told the hippogriff.

He snorted.

She wondered which of her readings had taken the foison out of the bars. They still looked solid and felt solid to a touch, but they weren't there when she poked her hand through where they seemed to be.

The unconscious guard woke suddenly. He scrambled to his feet and charged into the room, with his fellow guard from belowstairs just behind him.

Bradamant smiled at them both and tucked the magic book under one arm.

The guards saw a woman dressed in green, her long hair unbound, who lay down upon the air and flew out through a barred window, taking the king's fairy book with her.

Only a fairy could have done it.

When they had passed over Southwark, Bradamant made herself invisible again, with the last of the bitter potion, and added a sweet to take away the taste. Then the hippogriff turned. They flew back to the Tower and landed on the roof.

She had no intention of leaving behind the broken shutters on the floor below, evidence of a thief who broke in by means more like flesh-and-blood mortality, and not like the ease of the fairy magic that could send a fairy flying straight through bars of metal. Best not to let Cenwulf consider a difference between the thief's methods of entrance and departure.

The singing in the feast hall had stopped. There was a clamor of voices. Bradamant tied a rope to a crenelation and let herself down to the courtroom window. The same spell to heal injuries she had used on the guard mended the broken shutters, but sent Bradamant to sleep. She hung dreaming on the rope until the hippogriff flew past her and gave her a kick intended to be gentle.

She could not remember what the dream had been.

She pulled herself back up the rope to the roof, where the hippogriff landed beside her, with a soft whistle of relief. She gave him a hug and then climbed on his back and flew away to the north. The treasury window she left under spell. Cenwulf could always put real bars in on his own account. The void iron proved that fairy magic was responsible for the theft.

Bradamant gave the book into Lady Sylvia's keeping, and it was locked away in her strongest coffer and left in Bradamant's bower while they waited for Astolf's return.

When he came, Lady Sylvia wanted to bring him into the great hall to look over various matters in dealing with the estate. He laughed and kissed her. "I trust the steward, Mother. And trust you to watch over him. Where is it?"

"Very well," she said, reluctantly accepting his determination to see his book of magic before paying attention to anything else.

Lady Sylvia closed the door to Bradamant's bower carefully behind the three of them. She knelt by the coffer and paused, looking intently at her son. "He believed it? He thinks the good neighbors took it?"

"Yes."

She nodded and took the book out.

Astolf seized it and stood in a rapture, his eyes following the patterns of color or lack of color on the cover round, and round again.

After a while, Bradamant coughed and held out her hands to hold the book steady for him, if he would get round to opening it.

"What?" said Astolf. It took him a moment to focus his eyes on her. He laughed. "Oh, no, Cousin. It'll take me time to work out spells to find where you want to go. Let the book find you one place. While you go there, I can work on the others. Takes time—more now than before," he added, tugging at his beard, as he thought about it.

Bradamant clicked her tongue, considering his expression. The delay sounded reasonable by itself, but he did not sound as if he felt sure himself what he meant by it. "And when I come back you'll let me take the book to give to Oberon?"

"Don't know."

"Astolf!" said his mother.

"May not be ready," he said, but he added, "Isn't Oberon's, come to that. Logistilla gave it to me."

The two women looked at each other.

"Is this a good idea?" Lady Sylvia asked him.

"Don't know," he said again. He hugged Bradamant, and held her in his arms longer than usual, lost in his thoughts. Suddenly he let her go and looked at her in some confusion. "A little time," he said. He tucked the book under his cloak and left them.

In the tapestry, Prince Woden seemed to shade his eyes to watch him go. Prince Brutus looked quizzically at Bradamant. The eagle banner went on burning.

"I'll talk to him while you're gone," Lady Sylvia said.

"Well...." said Bradamant, thinking of how her own son reacted to advice.

"—and not too much," Lady Sylvia added.

Bradamant nodded and went to the bower door. Astolf was going out the palisade, to the secrecy of the wood.

The hippogriff, visible, soared in the sky above them, taking his daily exercise.

Chapter 4
The Dragon's Skin

In Le Rozier a new dairy was going up, with plenty of space for making cheese. The sheep and goats that pastured up the steeps of the limestone heights gave milk, said the townsfolk, of unutterable sweetness. Besides, with a good many years of peace inside the borders of the kingdom under Charlemagne, there was beginning to be time for putting up things other than strongholds.

Bradamant helped pass stones up to the workers on the roof, which was gradually rising beehive-round over the base. She had left the hippogriff outside the town to forage for himself, so that people would not be alarmed by the sight of him. The work went easily in the cool morning air. The day promised to be fair.

She thought that working on the dairy would in turn lead easily and pleasantly to asking about the trade that came through town of pilgrims on their way to Saint James, and from the pilgrim traffic she could go on to ask about the nearby shrine, and had the rueful Saracen returned there to guard it and was he still there. But somehow her questions fell flat. One youngster admitted to the opinion that Le Rozier made the best cheese for miles around, but her elders looked at her, and she did not venture any comment when Bradamant suggested that a new dairy would draw more of the pilgrim trade through town. No one in Le Rozier seemed to care about trade. No one seemed to care about pilgrims. Or at any rate, no one trusted a stranger in a mailcoat enough to say so.

It was true that Le Rozier was off the main line of the pilgrims. The best road went just a little to the west, through Millau and south over the Larzac Causse, not over the Black Causse that shadowed Le Rozier. The high limestone table-lands of the Causses were barren country, offering a little pasture, but no farmland. Their very barrenness made it easier to travel overland than to go by the rivers, too steep and swift in the highlands to be a useful guide. So pilgrims aiming at James's Compostello to the south went over the Causses, where the footing was easy, and the traffic spread out to wherever there were interesting shrines to visit and villages to offer guides and guards against bandits. They had a shrine, and there ought to be pilgrims heading into Spain, now that the road was open. Even if Le Rozier hadn't been able to get many of them before, why wasn't it getting its fair share now, and why didn't anyone seem to think the Saracen's shrine was interesting?

Bradamant worked a while longer, keeping silence, then said she was hungry. A couple took her into the shade of a chestnut tree, its leaves bright green above the blackness of its wrinkled bark. The two brought her a meal of cheese and nutbread and some of the local wine, mixed with water. She drank thirstily, for the air was growing hotter as the sun and the roof on the new dairy rose higher.

The woman said abruptly, "If you're on pilgrimage, Lady, you'd best ignore the chapel here. Go south."

"No, I mean to see the chapel."

The woman frowned, but her husband's face suddenly brightened. "Are you here to take care of the Saracen, Lady?"

The Saracen? So Rodomont was back at his shrine? That would explain a good deal. "What needs doing?"

"He needs killing, I think," said the man.

"—unless you could get him to go away home," said his wife. "But then we'd need to be sure he'd stay away. The other time he left, they said he'd gone to join the battle, and we thought he died there. But back he came with new scars, and up he went. Didn't seem to matter then. All he did was keep watch, peaceful like. But now— Lady, if he wants to batter everyone who comes near him, let him do it somewhere else. We have sheep and goats to pasture."

"Everyone?" said Bradamant.

"Everyone who goes up on the causse," the man said.

"But why?"

"Who knows? He started—oh—this last winter when the rains were so cold and heavy."

"No, he was getting odd and quiet before that," said the woman.

"No, that wasn't—well, perhaps." He puzzled over the timing a moment more. "Saracens don't all go off their heads when they meet with bad winters, do they?"

"No," said Bradamant.

"It's warm enough now," said the woman. "Can you help us, Lady?"

"I'm not sure. Maybe," said Bradamant, feeling confused. The villagers should have sent for help before. Evidently they did not much like their lord, and probably they'd hoped to keep their share of the pilgrim trade by not admitting that there was much the matter. That made sense well enough. But what did Rodomont think he was up to?

When he had first begun mourning Isabelle's death, his way of expressing it was to fight and slay all knights who passed by—a troublesome, but honorable way of expressing grief and guilt. Bradamant had beaten him in combat, and he had given up mourning to assume his command in the war against the Franks. Now it seemed he was back, and making matters worse. Bashing herders was no way to do penance.

Up on the causse it was hot. There were no trees there, and no shade. The tallest things growing there were the juniper bushes. Under the heavy gold of the sun, the juniper and the scrubby lavender bushes filled the air with tangy smells, as of things being preserved. Where the limestone came to the surface, the bald outcroppings swelled up, glowing many colors in the light: red and amber, white and grey and blue.

The grass was not as dry and slippery as it would turn in the high summer. The footing was not bad, and the broadbrimmed straw hat given her in the village helped against the sun. She climbed steadily.

When she came out on the tableland the stone stretched its colors out before her. In the distance she could see the little chapel with its tower and beyond it the towers of the city that was no city, Old Montpellier, the town of limestone crags, castles of solid rock.

The chapel was made of limestone, and inside lay the gilded body of Isabelle, who had tricked Rodomont into killing her rather than let him rape her.

Bradamant set out across the field of stone.

When she was halfway to the chapel, she caught sight of Rodomont, coming out the door. She waved, and he came running to meet her. As he ran, he drew his sword.

Bradamant frowned. "I just want to talk!" she called, but he didn't slow down. She clicked her tongue, drew her sword, and swung her shield forward. She didn't care much for his eccentric ideas of penance, if that was what he was still after. Better to get him home to Algiers.

Rodomont was not carrying a shield.

There was something odd about his pace. It was heavy, and a little slow. As he came nearer, she could hear his footsteps crashing on the stone, and soon she could feel the sound of them, shuddering in the ground beneath her feet.

The dragonskin armor passed down to him over centuries from the hunter Nimrod still shone bright blue and green. It glittered as he came near. Under the dragonhood she caught a glimpse of his face for a moment. It glowed dark amber, except for the grey scars, where her husband had struck him down in single combat in the war and left him for dead.

Something warned her—the look of his face, or the weight of his tread. As he swung on her, she leaped aside instead of taking the blow on her shield. His sword cut through air, and she could tell by the feel of the wind that the strength behind it was too much for a man. If it had landed on the shield, her arm behind it would have cracked. It was too late to run away from Rodomont.

She closed in to fight him, so that he could not strike a round, free blow at her with that unreasonable power. For some moments they traded blows, as he tried to go over or under her shield before it was raised or lowered against the blade.

Bradamant's chainmail was well made, but it was not invulnerable, as the dragonskin armor was. Any blow that Rodomont landed had a good chance of damaging her. She needed to strike him under the hood, or on the buckles of his armor, or through the hole she had made in his armor before, when she had the spear of Galafrone. She fought carefully, aiming her strokes with precision.

She got one buckle open at the knee, and next chance hit him there again.

The sword clanged against his leg and chipped off a fragment—surely not of flesh. Her hand and shoulder felt numb with the impact. For a moment she stood, gaping.

He howled in rage and struck her on the side.

Her armor held, but she was knocked off her feet and fell clattering on the hot stone.

He came running after, but she was too quick for him, rolling over and scrambling to her feet. His attempt to strike off her head as she lay fallen on the ground only removed her hat. He trampled it as he followed after her.

It was time to retreat. Back over the side of the causse? No, he might stand there and wait for her to reappear. Instead she ran toward the chapel.

Rodomont followed.

She leaned against the wall, midway between the corners, catching her breath. When he came around one side, she retreated round another.

When she went past the door, she could see Isabelle's coffin inside, carved in her likeness, and covered with goldleaf for her skin and hair, jewels for her eyes and lips and headdress. Dark lines of lead set off the sheen of gems and metal. It was expensive work. The craftsmen must have put many hours into making it.

Rodomont came round a corner again. This time she retreated beyond the chapel, to the gorge, a long, deep crack running through the limestone. A bridge of limestone slabs built over a wooden frame went across it. There were no railings.

She had just time to pull up the bucket that reached into the cold water running in shadow far below. She gulped down several mouthfuls of the bitter water. It tasted of the metals in the rock it had gone through.

Then she retreated to the middle of the bridge.

The last time she had been there, she and Rodomont had tilted, and she had beaten him, tumbling him off his horse and into the gorge. She wished they had horses this time, instead of fighting on foot like bandits. She wished she had Galafrone's spear back, too. How was she going to get through that armor without magic? Still, invulnerable armor would not help him climb out of the gorge if she could tumble him into it—preferably without being thrown over herself.

But Rodomont came running heedlessly onto the bridge. It creaked beneath his weight, but it was strongly built and did not give way.

Bradamant could not stand up to the charge, and there was no room to dodge. She fled, without even trying to trip him or slice at a buckle, and made for the crags of Old Montpellier. He could not match her speed.

Inside the rocks, in spite of the shade, the air was hot, shimmering between the bright colors of the rock towers.

Old Montpellier gave her an eerie feeling, on its own account, apart from the oddness of the game of armed peekaboo she had to play. Many of the stone buildings looked familiar. There were some like palaces in Paris, and some like tents in the desert. One was like the magician Atlante's castle of cold iron perched on a mountain. The boulder beneath it gave the replica a mountain of its own to rise from. And one was like Rodomont's chapel, tower and all. Were they really so much alike, or was it illusion, or had Rodomont been shaping it? It would be easy to get lost in the intricate corridors twisting between the rocks.

Rodomont came round the corner of the tall pink obelisk next to it, and she advanced to meet him. The "street" was too narrow for him to swing with his whole force. The little spear-hole was too hard to hit, but with the advantage of greater speed, Bradamant chopped open some more buckles. One blow landed on his knee, where she had nicked him before, but he did not seem to feel it this time. She got several of the fastenings chopped open before he realized he was losing and retreated backwards down the street.

She followed, still chopping at him. "What's happened?" she said, in between blows. "Why are you doing this?"

He made no answer.

The street opened out into a junction. Rodomont grinned and swung in a wide arc.

The blow fell on her shield and smashed her down against the square purple tower behind her. Bradamant rolled over and caught hold of a knob projecting from the tower to pull herself to her feet, leaving her shield behind.

It hurt to breathe.

She hid herself again in the mazes of Old Montpellier, stumbling and wheezing. She couldn't get enough air inside her to run. Rodomont didn't have the speed, but nothing seemed to tire him now. She stopped at last and leaned against a fiery pillar.

The heat weighed on her shoulders like a cloak. Colors wavered, glistening on the stones. She wanted another drink of water.

The pain about her chest grew easier. She must be badly bruised, but she did not think she had cracked any ribs. What she needed, she thought, was an advantage. What was there to work with? Stones, and cracks in the stones were about all there was in Old Montpellier.

She clicked her tongue and went looking for an aven. She had passed one or two already, but in the maze was no longer sure where they had been. The one she finally found was not, she thought, one that she had seen before. It lay at the foot of an amber minaret.

After a look up and down the street, she knelt and put her head into the aven. She couldn't see anything, but when she called out, the echo was enough to show that the hole underneath was large and deep. It was easy to understand how in old times people thought they led to Avernus, the old hell. She stood up and hopped cautiously. The stone quivered beneath her. Rodomont would not think that an aven led to Avernus, but he would still have to treat it with respect.

When he came that way, stalking her, he did not see her. She was up in the first balcony of the minaret, her bruises rather the more painful from the effort of the climb. He came near the aven.

"Hold still!" Bradamant called. "Stay where you are, and talk to me, or I'll jump." His weight put together with her weight landing from above would certainly break through the crust and drop them into the aven below. It would probably be harder on her than it would on him. She hoped he would not put it to the test.

Rodomont stayed where he was, and looked up at her.

"What's happened to you? Why are you doing this?" she asked him.

He stared up at her, and the hood of his armor fell back. His dull eyes were wide with astonishment. "To be safe," he said, forming the words with difficulty, as if he had not spoken in a long time. He thought it over, nodded, and thumped himself on the chest, as he repeated, "Safe." He thumped his chest again, thought some more, and struck himself with his sword across the knee she had nicked.

The sword broke.

"Safe," he said. He turned and marched away, back towards the bridge over the chasm.

Bradamant shivered, in spite of the heat. She did not like this magic, born of Old Montpellier and Nimrod's armor. She climbed over the edge of the balcony and went down the slender tower, groping about with her feet for the rough bits where she could get hold. The quilting under her armor stank of sweat, and the iron links gave off a hot, rusty smell. The muscles in her hands and arms began to tremble. She dropped the last foot, landing with a jar that rang in the aven like a trumpet out of tune. But the stone ground held beneath her.

She followed after Rodomont. He left Old Montpellier, and headed back to the chapel beyond the bridge. Bradamant did not try to catch up to him. At the bridge she took another drink of the bitter water and found a smaller rift nearby, where she turned aside to relieve herself, then went back to the bridge and stepped onto it.

Rodomont was in sight again, coming back from the chapel, but not alone. He was carrying the gold effigy.

Bradamant tried to hold the bridge against him, but he brushed on by, knocking her over with the effigy's feet, without bothering to try to push her over the edge. He seemed to have given up on the chapel he had built and the dangerous open spaces of the causse. He was heading for the replica in Old Montpellier.

She got to her feet stiffly and followed after him.

If he really meant to shut himself up in Old Montpellier, it would be small loss to anyone. He had been a disastrous king for his own people, leading them into war. Le Rozier had found him a difficult neighbor. He was her enemy. And yet somehow she did not want to leave him to the city on the causse. After all, there was her duty to Oberon. How would she retrieve the armor if she let him go? No doubt that was it.

She caught up to him and cut open the remaining buckles as they went. The coiled tail spread out behind him, undulating on the ground as he walked, and the cuffs flapped around his hands and feet. She tried to trip him, but without success. And all the while she kept trying to persuade him of the benefits of life. There were plenty of women left alive in the world, if not Isabelle, and there were gentler ways to woo them. There was his kingdom in Africa to rule. There were embassies to hear and speeches to address to them. He was good at giving speeches, or at least he had been. There were notable warriors he could test his skill against—not so many as before Roncesval, but she did not tell him that. There was a rosetree in Le Rozier coming into bloom.

Rodomont paid no attention, but flapped along to the duplicate of his chapel, in Old Montpellier. He stood the effigy against the wall and stuck his fingers into the crack that looked like a door ajar. He pulled, straining, and the crack split a little wider open.

"It isn't too late," said Bradamant. "Take off the armor and you can still be healed—I think."

He set the effigy inside.

Bradamant caught him round the waist and squeezed in between him and the wall to face him. Rodomont and the wall felt much the same. She put her arms around him and kissed him, trying to soften his lips.

Her feet went numb. Her hands were pinched behind him.

She let go of Rodomont and jerked her hands free.

Rodomont pointed to an octagonal castle down the street. "You could have one," he said. This seemed to be a generous offer. He seemed almost ready to be proud of himself for making it. Then he lost interest. He stepped over her shield, where it still lay in the street, and went into the chapel.

Bradamant stuck a foot in the door. He tried to close it, but the pressure did not hurt her, and he could not close the door with her there. He raised one foot, balancing himself against the darkness of the inner wall, to kick her out.

"I can move faster than you," Bradamant reminded him, although she was not entirely sure that was true at the moment. She tensed, trying to ready herself to jump with numb feet, if she had to.

He stopped and waited for her to explain what she wanted, if it was not a castle of her own in Old Montpellier.

"Take off the armor," she said. "You could still be—"

His chest moved slightly, as if letting out a sigh. "No," he said. "Couldn't."

He shrugged off the armor and dropped it on her. He banged one hand against the wall, with a boom that damaged neither. "Safe," he said.

Bradamant pulled herself and the armor free of the chapel. She tried to stand clear, but it was hard to balance on her numb feet. She fell, sprawling in the street, with the armor spread out before her.

Rodomont slammed the door, closing himself in with his golden Isabelle.

The door was gone. There was no break in the stone chapel's limestone wall.

Bradamant hitched herself out of the sunlight into the shade of the wall and sat up to pull off her boots. Her feet were grey and stone-hard. She wanted to scream, but was afraid it would hurt her bruises.

She forced her eyes away from her feet and looked at the dragonskin. She ought to call to Oberon to come and take it away from her. Old Montpellier was obviously a place of power. But she did not want to summon its powers. She could still hear the scrape of the chapel door closing to disappear.

Something moved at the top of the pink obelisk beside the chapel—moved and came slithering down, spiraling round and round the tower, and moaning softly as it went.

Bradamant stretched out and pulled her shield to her.

It was a dragon.

A pink dragon.

"Oberon!" she cried.

There was no answer.

The pink dragon stepped gingerly onto the ground, balanced her tail above her back, and ran on tiptoes to the skin.

"That's mine," said the dragon. Her French was clear, although the accent was peculiar, with a whistling, throaty tone. She had large, sharp teeth.

Bradamant blinked, too startled to argue this new claim.

The dragon stretched the skin out wide, then, with little grunts of pain, crawled under it and tried to fit into it. The head and front legs went in easily enough, but the hind legs and tail kept getting twisted. The dragon's delicate underskin was getting scraped against both the stones of the ground and the scales on the outside of the skin. The grunts turned to groans, and at last the dragon stopped, and peered out through one eyehole at Bradamant. The other eyehole had gotten hitched over the brow-ridge.

"Help me!" said the dragon, thought a moment, and added formally, "If it please you."

Bradamant gaped at the dragon. "I can't let a dragon loose on the world!" she said.

The dragon, with a little squeal, got both eyeholes into place and reached up one front claw, preening the ears into place. "By 'world,' I think you mean the two-legged creatures like yourself. Two-legged child, it was not the dragons who were loosed upon the 'world,' but the 'world' that was loosed upon the dragons. There are not many of us left. Help me."

Bradamant hesitated. "Do you promise not to harm people, if I do?"

"I have lived in terror of my life for more centuries than you can count, child, tracking after mine own—and I have survived, while dragons who thought themselves safe died. Of course I will not harm your people. Credit me with a little sense!"

"People say dragons are not to be trusted."

"How dare they!" The dragon gave a blurt of fire that hissed against the stones and died away, leaving an odor of sulfur. "Are those truly the stories you have heard, two-legged child? Dragons do not lie. Two-legs lie." The dragon shrugged. "Dragons only mislead."

"I've heard that," said Bradamant.

"I tell you: I will not hurt your people."

"But—what do you eat?"

"Meat, of course. But why bother with meat as dangerous as a two-legs? There are pigs on the earth, and goats, and wild-ox, and antelope, and elephants—" The dragon seemed ready to spend ages recalling the delights of food, but pulled up and interrupted herself regretfully, "—when possible. But it usually isn't possible, unless the elephant is old or ill, and not worth the eating. Even fish is better. Do you have any meat with you?"

"No."

"Will you help me?"

"And you won't harm people?"

"I will not," said the dragon, with exasperation.

The fact that Oberon had not appeared seemed to suggest that the dragon was telling the truth. Bradamant crawled over and straightened out the skin, then helped the dragon get tucked into it.

It was rather like getting her son ready to go outside on a cold day, when he was small. Of course, the dragon was larger than her son, even fully-grown.

She helped pick out pebbles that had got inside the skin and were chafing the dragon.

The dragon rolled over on her back, licking and smoothing herself like a cat. The slit down the middle of the skin kept pulling open, but each time the dragon licked it the belly scales held together a moment, and it seemed as if each time the moment was slightly longer. The long body twisted as the dragon rolled to lick the full length of herself. The scales flashed blue and green.

Bradamant, on her hands and knees, watched in fascination. A hole she had made with the magic spear was visible on one flank.

The dragon stopped suddenly. "Two-legged child, why do you go like the beasts of the field, and the dragons? Is that courtesy?"

Before Bradamant could answer, the dragon had thrust her snout forward and was sniffing at Bradamant's stony feet.

"Oh, I see," the dragon said. "You don't want them that way, I assume? Well, I am clearly in your debt and owe you a favor." The dragon let out a burst of fire. The flames played over Bradamant's feet.

Bradamant cried out in fear, but stopped. The fire did not hurt, or not at first. The heat began to hurt her legs, and she moaned. Then suddenly her feet were burning, and she screamed in pain.

The dragon's jaws snapped shut, cutting off the flames. The dragon sniffed at her feet again, swallowed, and coughed, giving off another whiff of sulfur. "Those burns will heal," said the dragon, and went back to rolling and preening. "Do you have such a thing as a gold solidus about you?"

"No."

"Never mind." The dragon licked the hole in her flank. "I have some about the right size in a hoard." The dragon rolled some more.

"How did you lose your skin?" said Bradamant.

The dragon stopped rolling to shudder at the memory. She scratched at a line of blue scales on her shoulder that did not sit right. "Have you heard that Nimrod was a mighty hunter, child?"

"Yes."

"Well," said the dragon, "He was." The dragon lifted her head, sniffing the wind, and then dropped it to set one ear against the ground. The dragon sniffed again, and listened again. "There are advantages," said the dragon, "to life unarmored—although not many." The dragon listened again and finally was sure of what she heard. "The villagers are coming to see what has happened. They will help you off the hill. Farewell."

The dragon was off, winding between the tall rocks, a streak of blue-green brilliance where the light reached her from the lowering sun. The scales flapped around the long belly, but without slowing the dragon's pace.

The air was a little cooler.

"Farewell, dragon," said Bradamant. She called once to the stone chapel, "Rodomont?" There was no answer from the seamless wall. She said a prayer for him and another for Isabelle.

She did not want to walk on her scorched feet, so she pulled her shield over, pillowed her head on it, and waited for the villagers to find her.

Chapter 5
The Ruby Shield

When he tried to spell the magician Atlante's shield to show its whereabouts, Astolph had a vision of Marseille, and a well, but before he could try to see in more detail, the vision faded from his mind. He heard an echo of drops of water falling onto water, and then even that was gone. Anyone who saw the shield's ruby light fell unconscious, and Bradamant's husband, thinking an unbeatable defense was dishonorable, had thrown it away when it came into his hands.

"That should do," said Bradamant. "I've governed there—I know the city." Finding the right well, given the right city, ought to be a simple enough task. Then she started to count springs, in and around the area, and it seemed a little harder. To the west of the city, near Arles, was the great plain around the Crau, where Hercules wept under the Ligurians' attack. His tears left the plain full of salt-water springs, welling up between the rocks Jupiter had dropped on the Ligurians' heads to discourage them from killing the out-numbered strong man. The Lacydon stream brought fresh water into the city itself. Further west were the marshes of the Rhone delta, and Bradamant made herself stop trying to count. She'd find it.

The garlic fair was going on, and the whole city had the smell of it. Bradamant had intended to head straight to the viscount's palace and ask for information, but with all that garlic to breathe she found her mouth watering and her stomach grumbling at her for fish-stew with garlic. Maybe she should get a wreath to take back as a present to Astolf and his mother—if the hippogriff didn't object—or try to eat it himself. Perhaps she had better plan to have a little extra to share.

Women stood in front of the tents where food was sold, shouting out their wares in the broad, carrying tones of Provencal French, coaxing and threatening the passerby to come in and sit down. Bradamant selected one where the smells seemed to match with the barker's promise of all possible varieties of shell and fish.

Inside the tent, it was dark, and Bradamant waited for her eyes to adjust. Suddenly someone was hugging her, calling her name. It was Marfisa, her sister-in-law, rising like her own phoenix out of the steam.

"So you're alive!" said Marfisa. "I thought you should be, if the genie played you fair. Come on, sit down, tell me everything!" Marfisa pulled her to a bench and called for more stew, and white wine.

The stew justified the barker's claims.

"What about you?" said Bradamant, two bowls later. "Is Isaac here, too?"

Marfisa coughed on a bit of shrimp, and said, "Yes, he's selling timber and buying wine and garlic. And he has a cousin in the coral trade here—he's staying with them while they argue over which pieces and how much. And you, my sister—still on the quest?"

Bradamant nodded. "I thought I'd ask the viscount if he has any idea which of the wells—"

"A well?" Marfisa interrupted.

"Yes?" said Bradamant.

"There's been trouble along the Lacydon. Some flooding, then some drought, then a lot of mud getting mixed in the water. And some wild-oxen were found the other day lying unconscious at the trough by a well that draws from the stream."

"What happened to the oxen?" said Bradamant.

"The viscount had them penned up before they could wake— and hard work they had of it, making the fencing strong enough. But they thought that would be safer than trying to sledge them somewhere else and risk having them wake as they went. He was going to butcher them today for a feast for the city for the opening of the garlic fair, but they disappeared during the night. The viscount slaughtered some of his own cattle instead."

Bradamant finished her last bit of crab. "Let's go look."

They came out into sunshine. Marseille was spread out above and below them on the hillside. Here and there outcroppings of chalk glittered white. At the bottom of the slope, the land kept going, opening out into the long curve that enfolded the harbor. The watchtower at the end was flying the city flag, as were most of the ships in port, a blue cross on silver.

Bradamant looked for the *Ramsbottom*, flying its lamb, but the moorings were too crowded for her to spot it. To the east along the shore lay the Calanques, the line of rocky inlets where ships hid whose owners wanted to try the risky business of trading in Marseille without paying the city's entrance fee. Hercules had tried to go through without a pause, when he drove Geryon's cattle out of Spain and round to Greece, getting himself ambushed by the Ligurians as he forced his way.

The next visitors from Greece had been more tactful, a band from the city of Phocaea. It had been Trojan property once, but Achilles captured it for Greece in the early years of the war. The Phocaean leader made a treaty with the people there and married their king's daughter. Together, the two groups had founded Massilia—Marseille. Provence was the oldest part of Charlemagne's kingdom, the first of the Provinces of the old Roman empire outside Italy, but its harbor Marseille was older still.

The bed of the Lacydon was invisible from where they stood. Much of it had already been built over, and the crowd of shops and houses on the slope hid the few open stretches.

As they went further from the harbor, the buildings became less crowded, and the stream-bed came out in the open. It ran mostly dry through the summer, damp sand on the surface, and the water in hiding underneath.

The smell of the garlic faded away, leaving at first the more usual city smells of human wastes and human crafts, and those in turn gave way to clean air.

They were far up the slope when they came to the well where the stunned wild-oxen had been found. It had only one house overlooking it nearby, a small house built of stones, with a mimosa bush beside the door. A young man and woman were sitting out in front, weaving cloth. They pitched the shuttle back and forth through the threads to each other, and paused at intervals to bang the cloth down tight. They were not Franks or Gauls, but a type she had seen before in Marseille, with noses very long and very straight, faces almost exactly oval. She thought it must be Greek, and indeed, seen one on each side of the loom, their faces looked like profiles on old coins. They were too engrossed in their work to pay attention to the women looking at the footprints that had trampled the ground beside the well.

"Too many to make any out, I'm afraid," said Marfisa. She knelt anyway, squinting at the tracks.

"I don't think it matters," said Bradamant. "I'd better look inside. Wait a minute—I'll go ask permission."

"I'll wait, but you're not going down the well unless that boy wants to help with the rope."

Bradamant started to argue, but it could not be denied that Marfisa was shorter and lighter. Bradamant grunted at her and went up to the hut.

"Is it all right if we go inside your well?"

"Not ours," said the woman.

"Whose is it?"

The weavers hesitated, and the man said, "Lacydon's."

The woman added softly, "No one'll mind, maybe. You can try."

"Thank you. Did you see the wild-oxen before they took them away?"

"Saw them soon's morning came," said the woman. "They must have come quiet in the night for the water."

"Any idea what could have done that to them?"

The weavers shook their heads, but the man said, "Lacydon, maybe. Not us."

Bradamant was not well pleased with their replies, but just then Marfisa gave a shout, and she let it go. There was something they didn't want to talk about, and the information that there was something to watch out for was enough to be going on with.

Behind her, the weavers bent their heads doggedly to their work.

"Can you hear the difference?" said Marfisa. She had lowered the bucket into the well, and she pulled on the rope to let it thump against something one direction and then another.

"I'm not sure," said Bradamant.

Marfisa tried again, and this time Bradamant could hear that one way the sound was muffled. "Might be just a stone in the lining sticking out at a funny angle," Marfisa said, frowning. "All the same—"

Bradamant nodded.

Marfisa shucked off her armor and quilting and stretched her arms up and down, relaxing the muscles.

Bradamant stepped back a pace, because Marfisa, in freeing her body, had freed the smell of the sweat with it, and it was a hot day.

"Never mind," said Marfisa, "we'll look for a bath-house later."

Bradamant nodded and took hold of the crank.

Marfisa turned into a shadow as she went down, and disappeared into the darkness. The splash and then the absence of weight on the rope told Bradamant that Marfisa was underwater.

For a few moments there was silence. Bradamant kept a hand on the rope and held her breath, straining to hear. Then splashes echoed up the well. Marfisa was straining at something.

She gave a cry of pain, choked off as water went down her throat.

There was a larger splash as she surfaced, coughing and wheezing. She tugged at the rope.

Bradamant set to winding up the rope, breathing in time to the crank so that the rope would come up evenly, without bumping Marfisa against the wall.

When she got her to the top, Bradamant caught Marfisa under the arms and hauled her out.

Marfisa gave a yelp.

She was holding something wrapped in weeds.

"Are you hurt?" said Bradamant.

"A little. Something jabbed my arm. Is this it?" Marfisa pulled at some of the weeds that bound her prize.

"Hey! Don't do that!"

"Oh. No," Marfisa agreed. "But, my sister, how can you be sure that's it if we can't look at it?"

"Let's worry about it later. Hold out your arm." Bradamant inspected the cut. It didn't seem to be deep. She bound it with her kerchief, while Marfisa held the weed bundle under her free arm. Then Bradamant held it while Marfisa got dressed. It smelled moldy.

Something bellowed from the other side of the hilltop. Startled, they turned and looked toward it.

Behind them, a voice said, "Good day to you."

They spun around. A sandy-haired woman, in a shimmering blue robe, was watching them.

She nodded very slightly at the weedy clump tucked under Bradamant's arm. "That shouldn't be left out in the open."

"We're taking care of it," said Bradamant.

"You could leave it with me to see that it gets returned," she said.

Marfisa's eye was on a shell-bladed knife the newcomer wore at her belt, although it could not be much of a weapon against armor.

Bradamant opened her mouth to call to Oberon, and see if that had any results.

The newcomer leaped forward and caught them both in an embrace, nestling their heads against her breast.

Then they were under water, unable to breathe.

Bradamant kicked and tugged, trying to pull free. There was no room for her to draw her sword, and she dared not try, for fear of striking Marfisa.

There was a pounding in her ears.

All she could see when she forced her eyes open was the shining blue water bubbling past her face. The pounding stopped. Something jarred solidly against them. The bubbles turned to white water in a flash of light.

She was lying on the ground, next to Marfisa, both of them gasping for air.

The sandy-haired woman gave one hand to each of them and pulled them up. "You fools!" she said.

"What?" said Bradamant, croaking like a frog. She clasped her arms tight, and found she was holding nothing.

The stranger flicked a drop of water at Bradamant's empty hands and made a gurgling noise of exasperation. "The ox-man took it! Bad enough he fouls the water, him and his wild-oxen, bad enough the townspeople keep putting buildings up over the stream, bad enough you dry-brained fools come grubbing just when I've found a good defense against them all—but you let the ox-man take it! Now they'll come trampling with their dirty hooves whenever they like, the beasts! and— What are you standing there staring for?"

"Do you have a better idea?" said Bradamant. Her voice sounded more like herself. This water-spirit, it seemed, had enjoyed having the ruby shield in her own keeping, and had been using it to make both humans and animals keep a respectful distance.

"Go get it back!" She pointed over the hills. Away from the well, the ground was too dry to hold impressions clearly. Wind had come up and wiped out most of the track. But there was enough to show the direction. The woman from the well leaned over and gave them each a little push.

Bradamant and Marfisa looked at each other, both skeptical.

The well-woman glared at them, sped to the well, let down the bucket, and pulled it up. It had a conch shell in it.

"That wasn't there before," said Marfisa, startled.

"One of you can stay here—you'll want to be sure I don't have it, I suppose. That's only sensible. But I don't. One of you go and get it—but call when you need help." She held out the conch.

"The wild-oxen drank here last night?" said Bradamant, scuffing at one clear hoof-print.

"What's that to anything?"

"When are they likely to come again?"

The well-woman started to jitter out another cry of impatience, but stopped abruptly. "Not tonight," she said. "Perhaps tomorrow. But they could go anywhere now if they liked, down into the city. No one could stop them."

"But there would be more people to try, and it'd be harder to get all of them," said Bradamant. "What do you think?" she asked Marfisa.

"We can't track them now. The ground's dry, and the wind at the top of the pass will blow away what's left of the tracks."

"Tomorrow." Bradamant eyed the conch shell. "Call if they show up tonight."

The well-woman's eyes glimmered in the light. They were as blue as her long robe. "As you say," she agreed, and sat down on the edge of the well. She propped her chin in her hands and brooded over the uncertainties of Bradamant's intentions.

Marfisa looked at the dusty path back to town, gauging the distance unhappily.

"We don't have to," said Bradamant, answering the look. She jerked her head at the weavers and started to untwist a silver link from her necklace.

"I have coins," said Marfisa. She looked up at the weavers' hut. "Not much room."

"Not much room in the palace, either, not with the garlic in town."

"True enough," said Marfisa, more cheerfully. A tramp in the heat of the afternoon after being stabbed and nearly drowned was not a comfortable prospect. A night on the floor of the weavers' hut was a better idea.

The weavers' names were Rhoda and Alexander. When their would-be guests offered payment, they were hospitable, in their laconic way, offering the best from their garden—fresh cucumbers and celery, and a squash baked with onions and garlic. After exchanging a look of question with each other, they brought out a silver cup for their guests to share. It was clearly their one treasure, and they were right in prizing it so, for it was very old. Hammered into its sides were pictures of Hercules. On one side, he goaded Geryon's cattle away from the ogre's stronghold, and on the other, the bandit Cacus, leaping down from a volcano to try to steal them away, fell beneath the hero's club.

The couple avoided speaking of what they considered the Lacydon's business, but Marfisa drew them out on the subject of how they marketed their cloth and which dyers they went to. The information would interest Isaac, too.

There were advantages to a refuge among weavers. There was clean cloth to re-bandage Marfisa's arm, and thin cloth to put over the door to keep bugs out, and thick cloth to heap on the floor for bedding.

Lying in the same room with a married couple made Bradamant lonely. She thought of the stars in the sky, to make herself sleepy, trying to place them correctly in their figures and remember their names and stories. About the time she began to wonder why Hercules was next to the Lyre, when he'd never been good at music, she fell asleep, and dreamed of the rain of stones falling around the weeping hero.

In the morning Bradamant and Marfisa examined the ground by the well, and discovered two dips of a reasonable size on opposite sides of the well, and off the path. They spread some of the weavers' cloths across the depressions, propping them up with little sticks to form low, unobtrusive tents. Earth scattered on top hid them fairly well.

It was hot, waiting in hiding, so they came out and went to lie in the shade of an olive tree. The sunlight was so bright and gold that the shadows were a deep blue. A starling scolded at them, but lost interest and fell silent when nothing happened.

They rested quietly on the grass, taking it in turns to lie flat with an ear to the ground. The well-woman might signal the intruder's approach before they heard him coming. Then again, she might not.

The weavers put their loom up behind the hut, where they couldn't see, but towards the middle of the day Rhoda came out, bringing them some food.

When she had set it down and been thanked, she stood waiting a moment, looking at their swords and armor.

Marfisa said, "What is it, my hostess?"

Rhoda said, "They're old, and they're stubborn." These did not seem to be quite the right words, and she tried again. "We're like family." She seemed to have it in mind to try again, but instead she gave a shrug and went back to the loom.

"What was that?" said Marfisa, who did not know the southern speech as well as Bradamant did.

Bradamant repeated the words.

"Ummm," said Marfisa. "I think that translates—try not to kill them."

Bradamant stretched out, her head among some stalks of yarrow, the white umbels of yarrow flowers shining around her like a ragged tiara. "I think the other way round is more the problem."

Marfisa sat up and dusted herself.

The shadows began to grow a little longer.

The sun was near the hills to the west when Marfisa heard heavy feet coming up the pass.

A high, sweet note came echoing out of the well at the same moment.

They packed themselves into their stuffy hiding-holes.

The herd of wild-oxen came over the hill, bigger and leaner than their domestic cousins. Their hair was black and glossy, shining in the light.

The ox-man leading them carried something draped now not in weeds but in a length of black ox-hide. He wore the mask of an ox on his head.

He looked around and gave a bellow. The wild-oxen gathered more closely at his heels, following him to water.

Bradamant choked back a gasp of surprise. The mask was not a mask. Its muscles flexed, its jaws opened without a gap or crinkle and revealed the ox-man's even, white teeth and pink mouth. The ox-head was his own.

They waited until he had reached the well and taken the bucket and rope into his hands. Then they burst out of their holes, scrambled to their feet, and raced at him, one from each side.

The ox-man let go the rope, and the bucket dropped into the well. He flipped the ox-hide cover back and turned to face Marfisa.

Bradamant saw a beam of fire flash in the air between the ox-man and Marfisa. The air crackled, and it smelt like thunder. Her ears hurt.

Marfisa toppled to the ground, unconscious.

The wild-oxen were bellowing in anger and confusion.

The ox-man was spinning, to turn the light of the ruby shield on Bradamant.

It was too late.

Bradamant was inside his guard, too close for him to turn the ruby shield upon her, too close for any of the wild-oxen to gore her without risking injury to their leader.

He wore no armor. His only clothing was a rough tunic made of ox-hide.

She turned the flat of her sword to strike down on his shield-arm.

His arm fell slack, but the shield stayed on it, for the straps were tightly bound.

He caught her round the throat, shoving his good hand up under the gorget. The big fingers closed on her. She couldn't breathe.

It was too close for swordplay. She rammed her shield into his belly. He let out a gasp and staggered, without letting her go. She rammed him again, and jumped to the side, in the direction of his stumble.

He fell, and she landed atop him. She brought the pommel of her sword down on his head.

He grunted and lay still.

It was not as easy as displaying the ruby shield, but the result was much the same.

Her own shield got in the way of grabbing his. She pulled frantically, first at her own, to get it off, and then at his. She slid her arm into the straps, and tried to leap to her feet, to be ready for the attack, but it had already come. She rose into water.

She knew she would not last long with her head beneath the waves, starved for air even before the well-woman entered the fight.

She caught a glimpse of her own shield on the ground. The silver fist and the red cedar wavered, seen through the water that flowed round her.

Something hit her. She thought it was the ox-man's head. The force of the blow sent her sailing into air.

She landed flat on the ground, half stunned, but with the ruby shield still on her arm. She thrashed about trying to stand up, or sit up. The magic fire blazed from her shield, striking many times. She put her hands over her ears against the noise. Then it stopped. The sharp smell in the air brought her back to herself.

Carefully, Bradamant sat up, and found herself the victor of the field. Before her lay Marfisa, the well-woman, the ox-man, and the herd. One of the wild-oxen lay almost beside her, breathing heavily, giving off a puff of fresh-grass smell at each breath. She supposed it had been the ox's charge that had pushed her out of the well-woman's grip. She wondered which of them it had intended to attack.

The sun was almost down to the top of the hills. Soon it would be too dark to see the ruby shield, except by its own light. And that light brought a darkness of its own to those who saw it.

The well, Bradamant decided, was obviously a place of power.

She got to her knees, and then to her feet, with some difficulty. Her head was pounding. Her back hurt from landing on the ground, and her breast and stomach hurt from where the wild-ox's head struck her. She was lucky not to have been gored. Her armor wouldn't have stopped those horns.

She tottered over to the well, and dug the silver chime out of her pouch. Free to the air, it rang in a breeze that rose from the harbor. Bradamant looked down into the darkness of the well.

The water rocked back and forth.

Hand over hand came Oberon up the rope. He swung himself out and stepped to the ground.

He ran his fingers over the top of the ruby shield, then untied his cloak and hooked it over the shield. The cloth was black, but it glimmered like silver, giving off a faint light, dull against the dark red of the setting sun. He bent over the ox-man.

The ox-man leaped to his feet with a roar that turned into a cry of pain.

Oberon straightened up, looking even more like a child against the ox-man's bulk. "That arm needs splinting," he said, nodding at the ox-man's shield arm. "Do you hear?" he said, more loudly.

Rhoda peered out from behind the hut. She dropped a curtsy to Oberon. "Are they hurt bad?"

"Nothing to worry about." Oberon held out his hand to the ox-man. "Will you come with me?"

The ox-man shook his head.

"You can't stay here forever. Look at all the trouble you give everyone!"

Rhoda and Alexander went into their hut and came out with strips of cloth and a bit of board.

"I won't leave my brothers." The ox-man's voice was deep, and slow. It seemed to be hard for him to find words or get them out.

Oberon perched on the side of the well. "You can't stay as you are."

Alexander held the injured arm steady while Rhoda tied it against the board and put a sling around the ox-man's bull neck to hold his arm still.

The ox-man knelt by the nearest of the wild-oxen, whispering into its ear to wake up.

Bradamant tried to clear her throat, but it hurt where the ox-man had choked her, so she clicked her tongue to get Oberon's attention, instead.

"What do you suggest?"

She pointed at the weavers.

"Do you think so?" He looked at them more closely. "Yes, perhaps. Advise us, my friends. What's to be done?"

Rhoda said to the ox-man, "The town keeps getting bigger. Romans and Franks and Saracens—people keep coming to settle here."

The ox-man helped the wild-ox to its feet and paused beside the well-woman's body. "We could drive them away."

"I don't think so," Bradamant whispered.

The ox-man said nothing, but went on to the next wild-ox.

Alexander said, "Your father laid claim to victory over all the land of the Ligurians."

The ox-man looked around at him.

"Go west to the Rhone delta—go into the marshes of the Camargue," said Alexander.

"Plenty of fresh water, and good cover," added Rhoda. "It'd be lonely, maybe, but it'd be safe."

The ox-man stood up. The wild-ox beside him rubbed its head against his flank. "I will go."

Oberon said to Rhoda, "Let me have a clue of thread."

She took a ball of thread from her pouch and tossed it to him.

He held it in his hands and sang something to it, looking into the west. When he opened his hands, the thread glowed faintly, a pale, silver light. He used one end of the clue to tie it into a corner of the ox-man's tunic.

"What?" said the ox-man suspiciously.

"To guide you home, if you ever decide you want to go."

"No," said the ox-man, and went on to another wild-ox.

Bradamant looked for the well-woman, and her eyes widened. "She's gone!"

There was a puddle of water seeping away into the earth where she had been.

a few houses—and the chapel Charlemagne had built. It marked his sorrow for the deaths of so many of his nobles and the site of their common grave. But it could also serve as a guardpost against the anger of the Basques.

Christian though they were, they were not Franks, and in hopes of throwing off their Frankish rulers, it was they who had guided the Saracen armies to the ambush at the pass over the mountains. But when Charlemagne had ridden into Spain to attack the Saracens by way of revenge, he had passed by the Basque villages, for the most part. After all, they might have sided with their neighbors to the south more out of fear of Spain than out of rebellion against the king. And the quantities of soldiers and supplies it would take to police a chain of mountains—and even then it would have been impossible to stand guard up and down every jag of the way—would have left other frontiers unguarded.

Officially, Charlemagne had accepted the submission and repentance of his Basque subjects. But he was glad of the flow of pilgrimages into Spain that made it possible for him to put up chapels here and there along the passes, staffed by clergy his schools had trained, and leave their upkeep to be paid for by the pilgrims' custom.

Bradamant landed toward the end of the afternoon, a little above the village, just below the crest of the path that led north, back into France. Below her, the narrow road opened into a wide, sloping plain, down to Spain. The ground below her was dusty in the summer heat, and the sight of the rocky ground there suddenly shook her with rage. It had been hard work digging a trench in that stony earth, to hold the bodies of the dead. Her husband had been one of the many to go down into the companionship of that long grave.

She urged the hippogriff into cover behind some boulders, and he obligingly settled down and was asleep in a moment,

Oberon did not seem to be surprised. He touched his finger to the water, tasted it, and nodded. After a moment's thought he turned to the weavers and said, "What about you? Will it be held against you? —for helping to recover the shield?"

"No," said Alexander.

"It's like water to forget," said Rhoda.

Oberon nodded again and slipped the ruby shield from Bradamant's arm. He wrapped it more securely in his cloak, then jumped up on the edge of the well. He flashed them a smile, and dropped into the water, leaving them in darkness.

"Lean on me," said Rhoda, groping toward her.

Bradamant discovered she was glad of a shoulder for support as they felt their way along the path to the hut. Alexander found Marfisa and came after them, with her in his arms.

It looked as if Marfisa was going to sleep through the night. Just as well, Bradamant thought. She was sleepy herself, even without a look into the light of the ruby shield, and she ached all over. She would tell Marfisa about their success in the morning.

but she could not at once relax to wait for twilight. Grudgingly, she prayed for grace to forgive the villagers. By the time her prayers were so far answered as to have left her feeling calmer, there was still light from the sky, but the sun had fallen below the slopes to the west. The ground beneath her feet was hard, but not rocky to look at, for it was covered with saxifrage, the starry little blooms shining white out of the mounds of stem and leaf digging their shallow, stubborn roots into the crevices. Over years, the little flowers would break up the stones beneath them, widening the room for other plants to grow.

Bradamant knelt, hearing a faint tinkling sound from the slope above her, and began picking a nosegay of saxifrage stars. Looking up, for a moment, she could see a flock of goats trotting down the hill, urged on by a goatgirl. As she would evidently not have the choice of being entirely unseen, Bradamant thought she might as well have some occupation, however trifling, to suggest a reason for her presence. The goatgirl would certainly not mistake her for a Basque, but might assume she was a pilgrim picking flowers as a courtesy to deck the chapel.

The girl went on by, and her goats after her.

The sky had been pink when Bradamant began gathering her bouquet, and was purple when she stopped. She snapped off a length of stem and tied the bouquet together.

She stood up, wondering if it was time to start up the slope yet, when a small commotion behind her spun her round.

It was a little flock of birds—cheeky and fearless in their numbers—objecting to the presence of a hippogriff where, by thrush and jay and finch judgment, hippogriffs had no right to be. They mobbed him, as they might have done an owl by daylight, diving on the hippogriff, one after the other, and pulling level to dart away again at the last moment with a shout of defiance.

The hippogriff flinched and squawked a protest at each of the first few dives.

Bradamant started to run back among the boulders to defend her beleaguered steed, when it occurred to the annoyed animal that he was, after all, much larger than his assailants.

As a thrush dove out of the sky, the hippogriff raised his wings once and brought them down, stirring the air, and throwing the thrush's balance off. The bird gave a cry, trying to recover. The hippogriff snapped at it with open beak, and the thrush dropped at his feet.

"Leave it!" said Bradamant, and with her arrival the other birds scattered.

The hippogriff stared at her out of one eye as if in wounded innocence.

The bird lay stunned on the rocky ground—dead, she thought at first—its brown and grey feathers almost invisible in shadow. After a moment she could see a faint motion at the throat. The thrush was alive and breathing.

The hippogriff saw it, too, and made a growling noise, evidently getting ready to dispose of the creature with one jab.

Partly to avoid more noise, and partly out of compassion, Bradamant dropped her bunch of saxifrage and caught the warm little body up in her hands. She stuffed it inside her mailshirt and the quilting beneath into her bosom. It should be safe enough there, and quiet, too. She waited a few moments to be sure it had air to breathe, feeling its breast move against hers, and its heart beat.

The hippogriff, satisfied that nothing more was about to attack, lay down with a sigh and stretched out. He pecked at the saxifrage idly, but found it not to his taste, and gave a snort, settling his beak comfortably over one leg.

Bradamant came out from the rocks sheltering the hippogriff and looked around her. The goatgirl's flock had reached the village. There was no one in sight, not even the gleam of cooking fires. It was the shortest night of the year, and the village had put out all individual hearths to gather around one big bonfire they would light to give new light to their homes. But she would be too high up to see when it began.

Roland's grave was not down by the village chapel, with the mass of the other dead from the battle, but further up. Bradamant set off in the shadows to find it.

At first it was easy going. She unfastened from the hippogriff the shovel she had brought and slung it at her back, then set off, following in the ruts of the trail. There was still some light from the sky, and the ground was open, making a wide, level space. Here her friends had fought and died, spilling out of the narrow pass just above. The track took her out of the plain and up into the pass, where the ambush had begun, with soldiers pouring out of the cover of the beech trees that grew on the steep slopes. The air was damp and death-like, and the walls of wood and scarp cut out most of the faint glimmer left in the sky. Soon it was entirely dark. She followed the ruts by feel.

When an owl hooted, she knew what it was, but the combination of the lonesome sound and the darkness made her feel frightened, even so. For a moment she stopped cold, and forced herself to concentrate on what was about her—the weight of the sword at her side and the shovel at her back, the warmth of the unconscious thrush at her breast, her feet scraping the dusty cart-tracks in the trail. There might be unfriendly goblins and frights about, but the magics they might bring against her would be small ones, and she did not think that any physical attack they could assemble against her would be stronger than she could manage, either. The greatest danger with a fright or a goblin was usually in giving way to the fear it inspired, and running away and so coming to grief through a fall.

There would be no ambush of soldiers dropping from the woods upon her.

It took a while for her pounding heart to accept this judgment, but the impulse to cry out and run downhill gradually grew weaker, and when she felt her feet were willing to take her uphill if she moved them, she started climbing again.

At last she came out from between the narrow walls to where the pass opened wider. The half-moon had risen by now, and the field before her was bright with silver, although the hills still rose high to each side. Behind her, the valleys were deep and dark. By daylight, she would have seen the glint of the Ebro, running far below her. Here Roland had come to die. He could keep watch on the road before him, in case his enemies realized that the last defender's strength was gone, and made a charge back up the trail. By then he could have done nothing to stop them, but he might have managed to blow another signal on his oliphant-horn to let the French on the other side of the pass know how close they were.

In the silver, colorless light, it was hard to make out the shapes along the road, but there were not many trees so high up, and the light was enough for her to find the marks she needed.

Many had thought that Charlemagne should not have buried all the dead there on the fields they had defended. All the soldiers—or perhaps at least the Twelve Peers—or perhaps at least Roland himself should be carried home to France. Many more, seeing the ornate monument Charlemagne had raised at home to the memory of the dead, said that Roland and the bodies of the rest of the Twelve had indeed been brought back and buried there.

Here was the milestone pine, with the four marble posts surrounding it to mark the compass. Roland had tried to break Durendal on them to keep it from falling into the hands of the Spanish. The marble was scored with gashes where the enduring blade had cut deep into each of the four stones. A little fountain bubbled up beside one, where the marble was cut through and down into the granite beneath. Bradamant knelt and took a drink of the cold water. Roland, probably, had simply been trying, doggedly, to keep his sword from capture, but Durendal was a thirsty sword, and would seek water, if it did not find blood. The dying man, after his climb up the track, was perhaps as ready to rejoice as to complain when Durendal, instead of shattering, had broken through to the spring.

And only a few yards farther along was the other pine, where Roland's strength had given out. There was soil around the pine, almost covering the roots, and in between the roots making a ground that was softer than the stretches of bare granite. With Durendal beneath him, Roland had stretched out on this last bed, and died.

And the sword had, after all, been safe beneath him. The Spanish troops, not realizing that they had in fact won the field, had broken and fled from Roland. For all they knew, he might—however improbably—have been shamming death and ready to rise and give battle if looters came at once upon him. And they knew very well that Roland had been able to blow his horn and signal for help. The thought of Charlemagne and the rest of the army pelting up the French side to the pass of Roncesvals, and likely to arrive at any moment, had weighed upon them, too.

The French had found Roland beneath the pine, and his sword Durendal beneath him.

Bradamant swung the shovel from her back. The thrush under her tunic stirred for a moment at the motion. Its tremor felt almost the same as it would have felt if her heart had skipped a beat, as it might have done in fear. And fear came into her heart, answering that sameness of motion, and she did not know how she could set herself to the task of digging into Roland's grave. What had seemed a reasonable plan by daylight—digging up a dangerously magic blade that Roland himself had meant to have destroyed, so that it could be taken out of the mortal world for good—seemed by moonlight an unholy grave-robbery.

Then she dropped the shovel, as the ground heaved at her feet.

The grave opened, and out jumped her cousin Roland, Lord of the Breton Marches, the sword Durendal in his hand. He gave himself a shake, like a dog just out of the water, except it was dirt he was shedding. With some difficulty, he settled Durendal into the scabbard at his side. He finally had to hold the scabbard up with one hand, and gave a little yelp as he pinched his thumb under the hilt when he got the blade all the way in. The links of his mail were rusty, and rustled scratchily about him. His tunic was almost in rags, although the quarters of red and white could still be made out as four patches of dark and light.

Battle training held her feet in place, although at first she could not speak. They stared at each other in silence. It was not a cousinly sort of welcome. But could the dead really be expected to remember their cousins? It might even be that he, too, was afraid—although she had never heard that the dead had any cause to fear the living. It was supposed to be the other way around. Especially, it occurred to her, the dead armed with a magically enduring sword. But he made no move to draw Durendal out again, and after a little she found her voice, and proceeded to tell him why she had come in search of his grave. She ended by asking if he would give her the sword.

He flung back his head and laughed merrily.

The laughter sounded like Roland's laugh, but it wasn't the reaction she would have expected from him to a proposal that he should give up his sword. It seemed odd, too, that he did not speak—could he have forgotten how? But she could not take time to meditate on the puzzle of why the March-Lord seemed so unlike himself.

He bent down, scrabbled about in the loose soil, and came up with a chunk of light-colored granite. It might have been pink-and-grey seen by daylight, but the moon washed out any colors. It glittered white in Roland's hands.

He closed his hands on it, grunting with the effort. When he opened his hands, she could see the marks of his fingers on the rock. He turned it over, showing how it was printed on both sides with his grip, then nodded with satisfaction and held it out for her to take.

A contest, was it? Surely he had not been quite as strong as that before he died. If she had known to expect a Roland, or something in his shape, that would bring a giant's strength and a giant's slowness in speech to his waking, she would have brought a good round cheese along with her. There were stories that said giants could be fooled by substituting something more malleable for this sort of test.

The thrush, waking fully, stirred, and pecked at her, irritably.

Bradamant choked back a cry and squirmed against the hard little beak, trying to collect her thoughts.

"Best two out of three?" she said. She held out her hands for the lump of granite, hoping that he understood what she had said and accepted it.

He dropped the granite into her grasp.

She caught it, with difficulty. It was heavy.

She closed her grip on it, to give the contest a try, but when she opened her hands, she was not surprised to see that she had entirely failed to mark it.

She heaved it back to him. "How far can you throw it?" she asked.

He flung himself forward and managed to snag it, caught off-balance, with a clumsiness that surprised her. Once he had hold of it, though, in spite of its weight, he tossed it lightly back and forth from hand to hand. Then he dropped one arm behind him and whirled it forward to fling the stone up towards the mountain that towered above the pass.

She could not tell in the moonlight just how far it went, but when it dropped out of the moonbeams into shadow, there was a perceptible delay before the sound of the impact as it hit the ground came back to them.

He put his hands on his hips and turned to her, with a look of self-satisfaction.

Bradamant knelt, pretending to hunt out a similar lump of granite in the earth, but instead reached into her tunic and eased the thrush out of its hiding place. She leaped to her feet, and reached into the air, letting go in the same moment.

The thrush took wing, rising toward the sky. It began to sing in its delight at finding itself free. Bradamant glanced at the figure of Roland to see if the song had given away the ruse, but he was silent, watching her missile with astonishment, but with no sign of disbelief.

When the thrush became too small for them to see it any longer, it was still rising. The song went on a little longer before it became too faint to hear.

Much as he looked like Roland, he could not be Roland. He was not a giant, though. He was tall, but not that tall—taller than she was by a head, but nothing like a giant's size. He was as trusting as a stone-headed giant, though. The real Roland would not have believed her. She had already begun to guess what he must be, as she drew her sword, saying, "Try a third, then. I'll fight you for it."

The Roland-figure tugged Durendal out of its sheath.

Neither of them had shields, but their swords were pointed as well as edged, and would lend themselves well enough to a fencing attack.

Bradamant flourished her sword in the air to test the balance, fighting without a shield.

He imitated the motion well enough.

She lunged forward, stabbing at his arm. He parried the blow and tried to cut at her head, then had to jump back, almost stumbling, as she took advantage of the high blow to duck and drive at him from under it.

He had Roland's height and reach and very nearly his speed. With those advantages, he was putting up a reasonably good fight. But he had nothing like Roland's grace and control.

Compared to the real thing, he was woefully uncertain of what he was doing—swinging wide, because he did not know how to get his full weight into the blow otherwise, and always too close to tripping over his own feet to be able to follow up on a blow that sent Bradamant back a pace.

He was too quick for her to go directly past his guard, whether she feinted up or down, to his back or to his front. She could turn his speed against him. He lunged at her, and she leaped back, instead of taking only as much of a step as was needed. He stumbled, trying to leap forward to take advantage of her retreat.

Bradamant side-stepped and brought her sword solidly down on his wrist—the flat, not the edge, for she had no heart to injure this bumbling creature.

Durendal fell from his hand and dropped, point first, into the ground, where it stood, trembling.

Her assailant was only a lamina, a clumsy sort of spirit that haunted the hills. The laminak were usually well intentioned, in their way, but so inept at managing the bodies they imitated or borrowed that they could almost bring down a house in their attempts to clean it. They could bring down a house entirely, and a whole village with it, if they happened to think of trying to cook on the fire.

"You stupid spirit!" Bradamant shouted at him, all the angrier now because he had started to cry, as laminak did when their feelings were hurt. "How dare you—how could you—you misbegotten, unbegotten, idiotic—"

That this bumbling creature was going around in the likeness of a human body—her cousin Roland's likeness, at that—seemed blasphemous. But before she could find words to give the lamina the blistering scolding he deserved, she was interrupted.

Something hit her—a blow from behind, felling her to the ground with such stunning force that it seemed as if the blow and the fall to the rocky ground must have left her with broken bones. She could not at first move her legs to rise again.

She could still see, though. Someone had run to the lamina and was standing there, arms around him, giving him comfort and drying his tears.

Bradamant gaped. The lamina's comforter was the goatgirl from the village below.

What was the goatgirl doing there? How could an unarmed girl, barely grown to woman-height, have struck her a blow like that?

The lamina had stopped crying. The goatgirl plucked Durendal out of the ground and put it back in the sheath at the lamina's side.

Bradamant tried again to move her legs and found that she could. As she shoved herself to her feet, the goatgirl spotted the motion and gave a chirruping call.

Something came running to her.

It was a billygoat. Bradamant was both amused and outraged to realize that the strength that had dropped her was nothing more than a butting billy at full speed. And the goatgirl, she supposed, must have heard the birds that tried to mob the hippogriff, and had stolen back up the hill, with the one goat for a guard, to see what was going on.

The goatgirl caught hold of the lamina's hand, and they ran away from Bradamant, with the billygoat frisking about to either side of them and obviously pleased with himself. They scrambled up into the hills, leaving the road through the pass.

Bradamant raised her head and looked at the ground beside her, where Durendal had fallen. A thin stream of water was trickling up from it. She inched over and drank from it, getting a sip at a time. Then she rose and started after them. Her bruises made it hard to make any speed, and in the moonlight it was hard to tell what she was seeing, in any case.

The lamina, leading the way, and the goatgirl and her goat after him, were rising up and up, without stopping. They must be following a trail. But when Bradamant tried to keep to their track, she kept missing the narrow line of trodden way and kept stepping onto loose rocks that took her skidding down again. It was hard to keep her footing and climb back again to the lamina's way, and harder still when she took a tumble to get to her feet again without sliding still further down. Her bruises kept complaining, and her mouth was dry again with rockdust.

She had just rolled to a halt against an uncompromising boulder, when she saw a light going by above her. It seemed to be following in the lamina's track. If she had not been so high up, she would have guessed it to be a will-o'-the-wisp, the madcap goblin that carries its cold fire through the marshes to lead travellers astray, and she would not have dared take it for a guide. But there could be no marshes or marshfire goblins so high in the stony mountains, and she crawled back up the scree until she came to solid footing, then set off after the light.

Once on the path and able to keep to it by following the light, it struck her that the light was very low—no higher than the ground, as far as she could tell. And it was very faint. It cast sparkles that flashed on the ground around it, but neither the gleam in the center nor the sparkles illuminated anything around them. And it kept waving back and forth as it sped forward.

She lost sight of it entirely for a moment when a wisp of thin cloud brushed over the moon. It was not really a light or a fire of any kind in itself, she realized, but perhaps a crystal of some kind, concentrating and refracting the moonlight that shone in upon it.

When the cloud passed, either the contrast of having the crystal's light back was enough to show her what it rode on, or in thinking about its undulating motion she had realized what must be there to see, and saw it because she looked for it. But in the instant when the light returned, she could see that she was following a snake—a magic snake, with a jewel in its head.

Some people, the stories said, had managed to steal such jewels and win a fortune by the theft. But she was not so needy that she cared to try her hand at fighting a snake that might or might not be poisonous, but was certainly magical. And it was the magic that mattered to her now. Surely, wherever the jewelled snake was going would be where the lamina had wanted to go.

The snake's way led her up a track of easier footing, on firmer ground. Even so, it took concentration to keep up with it, in sight of the sparkling light that gathered in and around the jewel in its head. Her bruises ached more as she went on. They were getting so high in the mountains that the air was thin, and hard for someone not bred to the hills to breathe.

The snake got ahead of her and dipped out of sight, but she plodded up in the direction it had gone. After a little, she came to where the narrow track turned down, and found herself coming into an open spot. She stumbled on something soft, and several more like it, before realizing that she was in a garden—an herb garden, she realized, from the aromatic smells rising up around her.

Ahead of her, the billygoat was quietly cropping something that released a sweet, nose-tickling odor. She had only a moment to take in what she was seeing before things began to happen so quickly that it felt to her as if it were a single action that occurred at a single moment in time, rather than a group of events coming in a sequence.

What she saw now was a towering dolmen built of three slabs of granite, and the lamina and the goatgirl looking into it. The goatgirl seemed to be arguing with the lamina, but she was speaking in the Basque language, and Bradamant knew only a few words of it. Beyond them to either side, the mountain sheered upward again. The dolmen itself was so tall that its crosspiece, seen from the garden below, ran as high as the hills behind it, but directly in back of it there seemed to be a narrow pass. She could see the sky through the portal, and a scattering of stars gleaming behind it. The snake nosed about among the herbs for a moment, sampling the scents and flavors cautiously. But then—

The snake, evidently deciding there was nothing worth lingering over in the garden, sped toward the dolmen.

The goatgirl either heard the faint sound of scales moving over the ground or caught a glimpse of the sparkles of moonlight thrown ahead by the diamond. She spun about, saw a treasure trove sliding by beneath her, and bent down to catch at the diamond.

The snake bent itself to one side, and struck, biting down on the girl's leg.

She screamed.

Bradamant jumped forward, sword out, and struck into the snake's back.

The lamina cried out and jumped back at them, landing a heavy blow on Bradamant's stomach—with his fist, luckily for her, as there was no time for him to drag Durendal out of the sheath. It was too hard for someone clumsy to manage all in the moment. If he could have freed the blade so quickly, the sword's thirst would have been satisfied with blood that time, not water.

Winded, bruised, and astonished to see the lamina protecting the creature that attacked his friend, Bradamant lay motionless on the ground, trying to draw a breath, and watched the lamina. He moved about his garden with a sort of clumsy confidence, looking as ungainly as he had before, but not stumbling on any of the herbs growing there, no matter how deceptive the light.

The goatgirl fell to the ground.

The lamina gathered a little bouquet in moments, then squatted down by the snake. It was still holding to its grip on the girl's leg, although it was writhing in pain. The lamina laid the herbs into the wound that Bradamant had made.

The snake gave one hiss, and then fell still.

Carefully, the lamina pried the snake's jaws open and picked it up, draping the shining head over his shoulder, holding the long body steady with a hand to either side of the wound. The rest of its length hung free, clearing the ground by a few inches.

The goatgirl tried to wrap the hem of her skirt around her bitten leg.

The billygoat looked up, inspected all of them, and turned a long gaze on his mistress. She made no call to him, and he seemed to decide that the others were none of his business. He blinked lazily, and went back to munching the sweet stuff on his side of the garden.

The smell made Bradamant sneeze, and freed her lungs. She gasped gratefully at the thin, dry air.

The lamina started toward the dolmen.

"Don't go!" said the goatgirl, speaking now in accented French so that Bradamant, too, could understand. She looked at Bradamant, apparently hoping that Bradamant had some way to hold the lamina.

The lamina hesitated, and looked questioningly at the goatgirl.

"The garden will wither," she added, but could not seem to think of any further reason to offer.

The lamina looked away from her and took another step toward the dolmen.

"What about Roland's sword?" Bradamant put in. "I won two out of three."

The lamina laughed merrily and stepped through the gateway the dolmen formed.

The snake's diamond flashed moonlight back into their eyes.

Bradamant blinked against the light, and when she looked again, the lamina was out of sight. She blinked again, this time not trusting what she saw. Beyond the dolmen, the cliff rose up as sharply in the frame of the uprights as it did to either side. The pass was gone. She raised herself to her knees, carefully, but the view of solid cliff beyond the dolmen remained the same. There was no sign of the lamina. "He's gone," she said, in astonishment.

"And it's all your fault!" said the goatgirl. "Who asked you to come and bully everyone? —just like a Frank."

A pair of angry answers came to mind, but Bradamant closed her lips against both of them. "In your village, you deserve anything that goes wrong" was not altogether true, strictly speaking, much as it appealed to her. "I am an officer of the king, and who are you to question me?" was true, but it was not her business as an officer of the king to go around saying things that would make people want to join in on any rebellion against the king that happened to come their way. Instead, after a moment's thought, she said, "Your friend was carrying Durendal around in the open. It's a dangerous blade."

"And you were going to take charge of it?" the girl said, with a skeptical sniff.

"No, I was going to send it back into the fairies' land."

"You succeeded, then," the girl said dryly.

Bradamant had been assuming that she had failed entirely in her hope of getting Durendal out of mortal reach and into safekeeping. Now she realized with surprise that the goatgirl must be right. The lamina had closed the door that went by way of the dolmen to an open ground no longer there. Such doors were not easily opened from either side, except by those with special skills in magic. What danger Durendal might be, if any, on the other side of the dolmen, in the hands of the lamina, to people there, she could not guess. But she did not need to.

The fairies had given the sword its unusual strength, and they could deal with it, now that it was at home.

She climbed slowly to her feet. The goat stopped eating and considered this development. Bradamant looked at the goatgirl attentively. No choking, no swelling, no strangeness of color, as far as could be judged in the moonlight. "It wasn't venomous?"

"No." The goatgirl looked down at her leg. "Is it still bleeding?"

Bradamant went to her and knelt down, keeping a watchful eye on the goat as she did so. The goat, however, went back to chewing on the bounty of the garden. The bite was bleeding, but sluggishly. The girl—Orosia, her name was—had a little knife at her belt for cutting up her food, and Bradamant took it and used it to cut off a bandage from the girl's skirt.

"Will he be all right there?" Orosia asked.

"I'd think so." Bradamant looked at her. The girl seemed to be trying not to cry. "Did you love him so much?"

"No! That is—" Orosia hesitated. "I don't think so. He let me graze the goats in his garden here. You've never tasted milk the like of it. And the cheese—!" She waved her hands by way of emphasis, not finding words for the excellence of her goats' cheese, but the motion hurt her leg, and she gave it up. She thought some more. "And I helped him learn to walk properly, and I was trying to teach him to talk, and he liked it. He was—well—he was my friend."

Or a long-shanked baby of her very own for a girl who was a little too old for a child's dolls, Bradamant thought, and not quite old enough to marry. Not, perhaps, a very safe baby, or a safe friendship. If this generous love had grown into something more passionate, it would have brought more trouble than delight. But it would probably never be clear, even to Orosia, and certainly not to Bradamant, if affection for the lamina might have grown into desire. Whatever it was or might have come to be, it had been sweet to Orosia.

"It surprised me," Bradamant said, as much to distract the girl from starting to cry as from genuine curiosity, "that he wouldn't leave the sword for me. I'd won it, I thought."

"It wasn't a fair contest!" Orosia protested, "You cheated."

"Did you tell him so?"

"Yes."

"I suppose that explains it."

Under Orosia's direction, Bradamant picked some of the lamina's herbs and bound them in against the snakebite under the makeshift bandage, then gathered others that they could eat.

The night was cold, even in full summer, so high up, but Orosia, with her injured leg, could scarcely go back down the narrow trail in the dimness of the moonlight.

Orosia called the goat over to sit between them, and they leaned against each other, back to back over the goat, sharing each other's warmth against the chill from the air and the damp ground.

The goat was inclined to resent this arrangement, but after some praise and coaxing from Orosia accepted it as tolerable.

Uncomfortable though it was, they were able to doze off, and sleep. It didn't feel like rest. It felt like sitting awake the rest of the night. But the way the moon went up the sky in jumps and started down again, still jumping, showed that there were long intervals of sleep.

When the sun rose, they got themselves creakily to their feet and set off down the trail, shuffling sideways to make a single line, as there was not room for them to go forward together. Orosia put one arm over Bradamant's shoulders, keeping most of her weight to that side, but getting a little support on the other side by keeping a hand on the goat's rump.

Once they reached Roland's grave, the going became easier. There was more room, so they could walk together facing forward. And Bradamant's abandoned shovel made a cane for Orosia. They went past the boulders sheltering the hippogriff from sight without rousing him.

When they reached the whitewashed walls of Orosia's home, Bradamant twisted a few links of silver off her necklace to give the girl's parents as payment for some cheese (for her own breakfast) and some grain (for the hippogriff). It was far too much, considered as payment for breakfast, and it was too little, considered as consolation for the loss of a friend, even an ungainly and doubtful one.

Orosia's parents considered it a rich noble's casual generosity, and thanked her with more courtesy than Orosia herself was able to summon up.

The cheese was, as claimed, the best that Bradamant had ever tasted. Hunger might have had something to do with it, but the goats that were milked for it had, after all, fed on the herbs of a lamina's garden. The sweetness seemed to give her strength again and take away the soreness of her bruises. She ate more of it as she mounted up the trail, bag of grain in one arm, in search of the hippogriff.

Chapter 7
The Ogre's Loom

White clouds rose in the east and in moments turned dark. Moments more brought an east wind, flinging the hippogriff out of his direction, although he tried to head himself north again, following the old Roman road beneath them. Bradamant wondered if she could get as far as Paris before the storm broke and take shelter there, but the wind grew stronger yet, chilling her in spite of her wool cloak. She gave it up, and touched the hippogriff's side to turn him west. Running with the wind would give them some time ahead of the rain to look for a town. They would be over Britanny before they could land. She wished she had her shield with her, as well as her sword, but officially there was peace there. Like the Basques, the Bretons had a language of their own, and were inclined to resent their Frankish overlords. But there had been no open rebellion in Charlemagne's time. Even when Roland, the warden of the Breton borders, followed the king's army to Roncesvals and died there, Britanny had remained quiet.

The hippogriff dropped to the side of a village built at the edge of a wide forest. The little houses were covered over with thatch roofs that went all the way down, slanting past the tops of the walls, to touch the ground. In the grey light, the houses blended in so much with the grass around them that Bradamant might almost have missed the settlement, except that the curve of open ground breaking into the forest line caught her eye.

As she guided the hippogriff in, she saw that one of the thatched buildings was considerably larger and taller than the others, and had a group of small buildings clustered at its side. This was obviously where the village's machtiern, or headman, lived, and she pointed it out to the hippogriff, who began circling to land in front of it.

A few people had already gathered to keep an eye on these strange visitors by the time the hippogriff settled neatly at the machtiern's front door and folded his wings to let Bradamant slide to the ground.

"Can you give me some shelter here tonight?" she asked, but the little circle of onlookers did not seem to understand her. She tried to act her question out for them, pointing first to the darkened sky, then to herself and the hippogriff, and then to the machtiern's doorway. But by then more people were coming out to see what going on, and one was clearly the machtiern himself. He was a young man, hardly more than a boy, with straight black hair over a bland round face, its lines not much changed by his attempt to grow a mustache. His rank was obvious from the richness of his clothing—a warm woolen cloak lined with Breton ermine, and a silk border on his robe—and from the way that others crowded themselves back to give him room to come through, with space beside for a couple of hunting dogs to plunge in next to him, ready to guard him, if need be. A tortoiseshell cat climbed into the thatch just above the door, and eyed the dogs and the hippogriff doubtfully.

He patted the dogs absently. "Who are you?" he said, first in Breton, and then in French, only a little accented. His voice was light, almost mocking, and sounded familiar to Bradamant, although at first she could not place it. Before she could answer, his green eyes lit with recognition. "Lady Bradamant! Welcome to the Forest of Broceliande!" he said. "You will want to stable your—your steed." He eyed the hippogriff with interest for a moment, then nodded at one of his men to attend her, and, with a bow, turned to go inside again.

She had placed him now—Nominoe, one of the many offshoots of the many lines of Breton nobles. He had been one of several hostages at the court of Charlemagne for the good behavior of Britanny. He must have been one of those freed to help keep the north in a pleasant mood when Charlemagne had gone fighting to the south.

The man told off to assist her looked as doubtfully as the cat at the hippogriff.

Bradamant put a hand on the hippogriff's neck and gestured to the stableman to show them the way. There was a separate building for the beasts, she was glad to see. Often, to save on building materials and fuel, people and beasts joined together in a single room—which was companionable, but smelly, and complicated when it came to mucking out, no matter how carefully they tried to keep the beasts penned on one side only.

The horses were a good deal worried by the entrance of the hippogriff, and the stableman had to go around reassuring them, while Bradamant set to rubbing down the hippogriff, making sure that feathers and fur and horsehair were all warm and dry before she gave him a pail of water and a measure of oats, and a parting embrace, and went to her own shelter.

The rain had begun falling in earnest as the stableman led her back to the main building. Even without the company of the beasts, it was stuffy inside, for there was no proper chimney, only a stone-paved square in the middle of the room, with a fire burning fitfully, and a smokehole above. The rain and the winds meant that the smoke kept shifting about in the room.

Nominoe evidently considered it beneath his dignity to leave his chair or try to shuffle it about across the floor when the smoke came his way. The result was that he and those in conversation with him kept having to interrupt themselves by stopping to cough. Others less favored by rank shifted about to other benches or stools or places to stand as the wind changed, and so avoided the worst of the drifting ash. The dogs and the cat seemed to have been brought up together, for they were friends, and snuggled in a warm heap at the feet of any sympathetic person who happened to be out of the smoke at the moment.

Nominoe was nibbling cheese and drinking a horn of yellow wine. Someone brought a bowl of soup for Bradamant and another horn of wine.

"So you have come to visit perfidious Britanny, my lady," Nominoe said lightly.

Bradamant tried to laugh politely at this barbed pleasantry. Charlemagne and his officers did in truth consider Bretons perfidious. The Bretons regularly broke the treaties that had been imposed upon them by force, then disappeared into the forests when armies came to recall them to their sworn oath. "I'm not here on the king's business, my lord," she told him.

"As you say, my lady," he agreed, without sounding as if he believed it.

"No, I've been on a quest."

"For a hippogriff? My congratulations, then."

"No, for talismans that the fairies gave us in the war against the Saracens."

"To give to the king?" he asked, raising his eyebrows.

"To the fairy king." She would have been willing, in any case, to tell him about her search for talismans, but she was glad, besides, for an excuse to avoid discussing treaties between King Charlemagne and Breton lordlings.

When she was done, Nominoe refilled her horn with wine and was silent a moment, patting one of the dogs. Then he said, "So you are in favor with the good neighbors, my lady?"

"That's a bolder claim than I'd care to make, my lord." She looked at the boy again. "Why? —do you know of a talisman around here?"

"Broceliande is full of stories of wonders, my lady. You would need to take rollers to almost every stone and an axe to every stick in the wood to get all the magic out of it. But talismans such as a mortal might claim to own and hand over or fight to keep as he might choose—I have not heard such a story as that about us. And yet we are rich in stories here."

"Do you have a particular story in mind, my lord?"

"The story of the devil-born owners of the Castle of Worst Luck," he answered.

"I don't know that story," she admitted.

He clicked his tongue at such ignorance and tried again. "Do you know who King Arthur was, my lady?"

"He was the sleeping wizard's king."

Nominoe looked taken aback at this way of putting it. "You know of the wizard Merlin, then."

"The good sorceress Melissa, before she passed on, took me to hear an oracle from him."

Nominoe's eyes widened in awe at these connections, but he could not comment just then, because the wind shifted, and they coughed and shivered as a gust of wind got past the smoke-hole's rain-shield and swept down on them.

"King Arthur's nephew Yvain," Nominoe said meditatively, once the wind had shifted again, "once came to Broceliande and won himself a bride and a castle here, the story goes."

"The Castle of Worst Luck?"

"A castle of better omen and greater comfort than that," Nominoe said. "But he conquered the devil-spawn who had been kidnapping maidens from all the country round to keep prisoners in their castle, cold and ill-fed, slaving at their looms for them, spinning silk, and who knows what drudgery, besides—" He paused, by way of emphasizing the importance of what he had next to say. "One at least of the devil-spawn has come back to the Castle of Worst Luck—and there are maidens missing!"

"What do you mean by 'devil-spawn,' my lord," Bradamant asked cautiously. "Evil humans, or are they monsters of some kind?"

He started to say "Monsters," then paused to consider a moment. "I suppose there are humans who do as much evil as monsters," he said thoughtfully.

"As much—and more of us to do it," she reminded him.

"I might even say it was an evil deed when King Charlemagne kidnapped me, my lady," he said dryly.

"You might, my lord, but I don't think that you were ill-fed or ill-clad—if not perhaps in ermine—or set to drudgery, unless you count learning to read in the royal school."

Nominoe's quick smile flashed at her. "I did not count reading drudgery," he admitted.

She waited, while he considered the matter closer to hand.

At length he said, "They are shaped like humans, so I've heard, but they are crooked and stooped and hairy, and their heads are peculiar. They have long drooling tusks and great jutting brows that shadow their faces so deeply you can't tell if they have two eyes, or one great one filling the shadow, or none at all."

Bradamant blinked. She had heard a description like that before.

Nominoe, catching the change in her expression, leaned forward intently. "What are they?" he demanded.

"They are land-orcs—ogres. They're not like the great sea-orcs. Those are a kind of beast owned by the merfolk. The land-orcs are more like people, in shape, in spite of their hairiness. And they can speak, I think. The King of Damascus never heard the one speak that kidnapped his bride. But the ogre had a woman—a human woman he kept as his wife—who begged him to let the lovers go, so I suppose he understood speech."

"And did he let them go?" Nominoe asked.

"No. But while the ogre was guarding the pathway to the women he had stolen, to keep the King of Damascus from coming up, his friend the King of Tartary managed to climb the steeps of the hill from behind and rescue her that way. The ogre fell from the ridge down among the rocks trying to go after them and was never seen again. They rescued the women he'd been keeping prisoner in the caves and brought them home."

One of the dogs yelped as Nominoe gripped its ears too hard. He gave up petting it and clasped his hands in front of him on the table. Besides the more obvious reasons that males might have to kidnap females, Nominoe was no doubt considering the possibility of a horrible death. Ogres, so it was said, ate people. Yvain's ogres, by his account, had not killed their captives. And the story that had come back from the King of Damascus had said that the land-orc kept women alive, for purposes not explained. But he killed and ate all human men who fell into his hands, like the Cyclops in the old stories that Nominoe—having been well taught in his years as a hostage—undoubtedly remembered. Then again, overwork and cold and hunger could kill people, too, and though such a death might revolt the hearers less, it was no improvement considered from the victim's point of view. A human male who collected and imprisoned women would surely be accused of raping them, and no doubt the boy was facing up to this possibility, as well, although neither story spoke of it.

Bradamant told herself that when she next saw King Charlemagne, she should tell him that he owed her a favor for being of considerable diplomatic service to him. Aloud, she said to Nominoe, "Perhaps I could be of assistance."

Some of the tightness went out of his hands and shoulders. Going up against an ogre alone was a formidable prospect. He said with careful formality, "I would be grateful, my lady."

By then the rain had grown softer. The wind had fallen, and the fire was burning easily. Soon the gathering broke up. The hall was not so much larger than the rest of the homes in the village as to have much in the way of guest quarters. Bradamant found herself assigned to a couple with room to take in a visiting woman. They spoke no French, but made her welcome with gestures, and she answered the same way. They had a single daughter, and the half of her bed was the family's extra space. The girl courteously took the wall-side, leaving Bradamant the easier side for getting to the chamberpot in the night if needed. She did not take advantage of this courtesy, however, as hippogriff-riding in high winds, with scant sleep the night before, had tired her out. She slept the night through, waking only partway, once, from a nightmare of meeting a hungry land-orc. She lay still, glad of the silent warmth of the sleeping girl beside her, and let the image of blind, groping hands fade from her mind, until sleep took her down again.

In the morning, she met Nominoe at his hall. He wore a mailshirt, leather leggings and helmet, and carried a shield of leather-covered wood, with an ermine-tails pattern of black spots painted on the leather, as well as an extra shield, unpainted, for Bradamant's use. The French had tried to keep the Bretons from easy access to supplies of metal, but could not keep them from the protection of leather.

With him was one of his followers, a young man called Marrec, with much the same equipment, except that he had no mailshirt, but only a leather jerkin. It seemed a small band for hunting ogres. Bradamant looked at Nominoe questioningly, who shrugged. "They're afraid of the ogre," he said. "I could order more to come, but I don't think they'd obey, and I don't want them to get in the habit of thinking I'm a tyrant if I forced them, and a weakling if I didn't."

Bradamant nodded, accepting the boy's judgement. He might be young, but he evidently understood both his power as a leader and its limits. "You are braver than most," she said to Marrec, but he didn't know French, and shook his head, with a blank look.

"His wife is one of the missing." Nominoe put on his handsome ermine-lined cape, although the day promised to be hot.

Marrec went ahead of them with an axe and chopped a way into the forest. A path led in, but briars and thorns grew quickly at the border between supporting trees and sunlight, and it had been some time since the path was used last. It was marked by a line of stones on each side, and the entrance was not entirely grown over, but it was thick enough to make the assistance welcome. Thorns could work their way through mail and tear through leather.

The forest was mostly pine and beechwood, although in places oak was taking over. The branches with leaves spreading above

them and the branches with needles spreading beside them kept
out all sunlight. Mail and leather were no longer uncomfortably
hot. It was hard to see.

The thorny vines disappeared. There was not enough light
inside Broceliande for them to grow. With a little shiver of relief,
Marrec squeezed himself to one side of the path and let Nominoe
and Bradamant take the lead.

At first, there was no chance of missing the way. Small
stones, and then a double row of standing stones led them
straight through the shadows. They went in single-file, as the
path was narrow. After an hour's silent walking they came to
another thorny patch. Marrec took his axe to the briars, and
they struggled through to find themselves at the edge of a pool
of water bubbling up from a spring.

Nominoe hesitated, and consulted with Marrec. There were
several tracks opening into the pines that surrounded the pool,
but none kept up well enough to be clearly the work of people with
a fixed destination. Some could have been trails left by animals
coming to drink. The shore had once been banked up, and could
still be walked on, but it was gradually turning marshy. The
end of the stone-guarded path that had brought them there had
once been marked by a wide, heavy step-stone, its imprint still
visible on the bank, but the stone itself was gone.

After discussion, and much peering into the various openings,
Marrec offered a recommendation which Nominoe accepted.
They oozed themselves one at a time over the marshy edge of
the pool to a trail that took them away from the shore, and set
off into the darkness of the pines again. Marrec led the way
now, anxiously nicking cuts into the resiny bark wherever they
had to make a choice of ways. Neither Marrec nor Nominoe was
sure of their path, and they had to turn and come back more
than once when a trail lost itself in the woods. But they did not
come all the way back to the pool, so Bradamant supposed that
between them they had explored the woods enough—perhaps
before the reports of the ogre's return to Broceliande—to know
well enough what they were about.

Marrec's burden of supplies included a bag with a loaf of
bread and a leather bottle of wine. When their stomachs began
to grumble, he started breaking off chunks of the bread, and

they passed the wine from one to another until both wine and bread were gone. They thought it was a little past noon by then, although with the heavy pines, it was hard to see the sun, and the twisting of the forest trails made it hard to judge directions.

It might have been an hour later when the pines gave way to beech, and another hour when the beechwoods gave way to fruit trees. They were spaced thinly enough to let in patches of gold, dazzling their eyes. There was not quite enough light for another barrier of vines, and they made their way slowly between the new trees, letting their eyes adjust.

The fruit loading the branches looked something like dark purple blackberries, if blackberries had been stretched long and thin. Birds were busy in the branches eating the berries, stopping only to whistle their approval at one another every now and then.

"Are those good to eat?" Bradamant asked, in some curiosity.

Nominoe passed the question on to Marrec, who told them that when he had tried the berries, he had been thirsty, and relished their juiciness, but they didn't have much flavor.

Bradamant and Nominoe tried a couple, and agreed with Marrec's opinion.

"And the ogre's stronghold is in this grove?" Bradamant asked.

Marrec said he had felt too much afraid, when he found himself in this stand of trees he did not recognize, to explore farther before, but he had caught sight of grey stones before he turned back, and believed them to be part of a wall.

They went more slowly, now, in order to move as soundlessly as they could through the grove. Although they weren't running into thorns, there was light enough for tall grasses to grow, and burrs among them. After a little while, the full-grown trees gave way to ground that looked more open, because the trees were smaller, row upon row of them with the center branches pruned away, so that all the remaining branches grew low, spreading out wide and bushy, instead of tall and thin. The grass and weeds had been scythed.

They stopped to pick the burrs off each other and look about them. Rising above the bushy rows ahead, the stone wall Marrec had glimpsed before was just visible, glinting a little with bits of mica in the light.

After they had passed a few more trees, they caught sight of a human being, a young woman reaching in beyond the berries to pluck something they could not see from their distance off from the inner branches.

For the captive of an ogre, the woman seemed to be remarkably free of guard and remarkably unconcerned with thoughts of escape. Her body was healthily plump, and obviously not subject to starvation. Her dress was not ragged in the least, but was made of a sheeny cloth that looked like silk as fine as any Isaac imported from Damascus and the Silk-lands of the far East, and silk all over, not just a border. It was patterned with a design of horse-tail reeds in dark green and light green against a sunny yellow ground.

Keeping to the cover of the bushes between them and the woman in reeds, they continued silently toward the stone wall. After a little they came in sight of an entryway. Through it they could see the ogre standing, leaning on a crooked staff as in meditation. They stopped, half in caution and half in dismay that they had really found the fearsome figure they sought.

Seen from the side, the ogre's brow ridge stood out sharply against the grey stone of the inner wall curving behind. The ogre would have been tall, standing straight, but was stooped, and so perhaps no higher than Nominoe. The ogre wore what looked like a long, white robe.

A red-headed woman, dressed in bright autumn-leaf silks that echoed the color of her hair, was sitting on a stone bench behind the ogre, drawing designs onto a wax tablet.

Before they could edge enough to the side to put themselves out of sight of the entryway, a cuckoo landed on the bush above them, cocked an eye at them, and gave out its cheerful, mocking cry. It startled all of them, including the ogre, whose head snapped round in their direction at the cuckoo's note.

The ogre let out a low growl.

The robe of white dissolved and turned into a cloud of butterflies or moths, rising into the air and away. The ogre's own clothes, hidden until then, were revealed as a silk robe like the ones the two human women wore, with a pattern of purple berries and green boughs like the ones in the grove around them.

The cuckoo took off after the frightened cloud of insects.

Nominoe, with Bradamant and Marrec at his heels, dashed for the gateway, hoping to get through before the ogre could bar the door against them.

The woman outside the gate cried out in fear and, instead of running away to freedom, snatched up the bag she had harvested and made for the gateway.

The red-headed woman caught up her tablets, clutching them to her breast, and leaped to her feet. "Marrec!" she said.

Then the three of them were through the gateway. The youngster with the sack made it through just behind them and swerved away from them, along the inner line of the wall.

The ogre, although not in time to stop them from entering the grounds, was not daunted by facing three of them. The ogre twirled the long staff once as if it had been a light baton, and brought it down on Marrec's shoulder.

Marrec fell and could not get up.

The woman in reeds, her bag slung over her shoulder, kept on running, and made for the castle door.

Bradamant and Nominoe moved a little apart to come at the ogre from two sides.

The ogre backed up against the wall so that they could not come from completely opposite sides.

The red-headed woman bit at her lip, watching the ogre wait for the remaining two assailants to move in. Then she set her tablets on the ground and—making a wide curve away around the fight—ran to see how Marrec was. She knelt beside him.

Bradamant and Nominoe exchanged a glance, and she cut at the ogre, pulling back more swiftly than she had expected to need to do from the return blow, and Nominoe struck from the other side. But the ogre turned and turned again, holding both of them off.

Fighting so close, they could see that the ogre had two eyes, after all, gleaming from under the shadow of the brow-ridge.

The ogre might be stooped, but was both fast and long in the arm. The staff was made of cornel-wood, and reinforced with copper at both ends. Even without a sword's edge to it, it was a formidable weapon so wielded. They were two against one, and the ogre had no shield, but for long moments the fight seemed like an exercise, with no blows landing and, as it seemed, no possibility of getting any to land. It might have been a game, marked only by a slow, crab-like progression along the face of the wall, as Nominoe, with the shortest reach of the three, stepped away from the ogre.

The ermine markings on Nominoe's shield began to look streaked, instead of spotted, as the staff scraped over his shield.

Sparing a glance for her partner, Bradamant saw at length that he was breathing hard, even though he was still moving as quickly as before. Soon he would have to slow his pace. She tried to quicken hers, to get in a blow before that could happen, but the ogre gave a deep chuckle and struck her sword aside all the faster. Bradamant had to step back herself to keep the heavy staff landing on her shield, not directly on either herself or her blade.

The ogre made use of that half-moment as Bradamant shifted back, to strike at Nominoe's legs beneath his shield. Nominoe brought his shield down hard, hitting the staff. Done with a metal shield, he might have been able to trap the ogre's staff against the ground, but the blunter wood-and-leather edge could not do that. The ogre, leaning in, slid the staff between his feet, and hooked his legs out from under him. He fell with a crash to the ground.

The ogre roared approvingly.

But then Bradamant had stepped forward again, and the ogre had to give attention to her. Nominoe had a moment clear to roll over and scramble to his feet.

The ogre yelled as the blade cut into flesh. The ogre pulled back, gaining room to swing twice, once at Bradamant, without connecting, and once at Nominoe, shoving him back.

Bradamant, trying for another cut, swung with full force. The ogre dodged, and Bradamant's sword rang against the wall with too much force for her to hold it as stones brought the swing to a halt. The sword bounced from wall to grass, by good fortune unbroken. Her hand stung so keenly that she was not sure if she had been as lucky.

The ogre's staff swung up again, revealing a long slice in the silken robe, with blood from the cut already discoloring the fabric beneath, and also—

Bradamant gaped.

"Hold!" someone called, from the castle door, once in Breton and again in French.

The ogre pulled to a halt, staff still up in the air, ready to land another blow.

Nominoe swung around, limping a little, to face the women at the door.

Bradamant considered the distance to where her sword lay on the grass, but it was too far. She left it alone and turned to the castle.

Two young women stood in the doorway, one the woman in autumn-leaf silks who had recognized Marrec, and the other, the one who spoke both Breton and French, a newcomer, dressed like the other in silk. Her robe was woven in a pattern of willow-trees. She said something to her companion, who turned and ran back into the hall.

The willow trees shifted on the newcomer's robe as if in a wind, as she came running down the steps. Nominoe held out his arms to her. But she stopped short of his embrace, looking him over, evidently thinking that he might have suffered some injury and fearing to make it worse if that were so.

Just then the ogre made some small noise, and the woman in willow, still looking at Nominoe even as she moved, went to the ogre.

The ogre was growing pale with loss of blood. The willow-woman eased the ogre down to the ground and crumpled a double handful of the loose fabric of the ogre's robe to make a pad to bunch against the blood flowing from the cut of Bradamant's sword. The blood was spilling smoothly, not bursting in time to the heartbeat, and the ogre was breathing easily, with no bloody froth forming at the lips. It was a wound likely to heal well.

The ogre stirred, trying to rise up and resume the interrupted battle, but the woman in willow made hushing noises, and then, when the ogre still struggled to climb free, said something in a solemn voice.

"You cannot promise that for me!" Nominoe exclaimed.

"Lord Nominoe, you will surely not attack one who is injured and fallen," she replied.

The ogre looked balefully at Bradamant, but had stopped trying to get up.

"I think for the moment, we have all agreed to a truce," Bradamant said carefully, and the woman in willow repeated her words to the ogre in Breton.

Meanwhile, the autumn-leaf woman had returned, with a pail of water and scraps of cloth suitable for bandaging, and pulled down the ogre's robe to start binding the cut.

Nominoe stared in astonishment, turned red, and forced his gaze away from the hairy, curving breast revealed before him. "That's a woman!" he said angrily.

Bradamant dipped her hand in the water. It still hurt a good deal, but she began to feel sure it was not broken. "So am I," she reminded him. Having glimpsed the breast of the ogre—of the ogress—through the rent she had opened in the robe, Bradamant had already realized what Nominoe was now first seeing.

Nominoe took refuge in courtesy and introduced them to one another. The red-headed woman in autumn leaves was Marrec's wife Acfrud, and the plump young woman in reeds was Duoda. The willow-woman was Arganthael. Nominoe did not say that Arganthael was his betrothed, but Bradamant could see in their faces that it was so. And the ogress, Arganthael told them, was known to them from the bushes in her grove as Mulberry.

Nominoe gathered up a share of the bandages and went to Marrec's side, with a nod to Bradamant to assist him, and they fashioned a sling to hold Marrec's arm still. He was in a good deal of pain, with a broken clavicle, but was able with their help to rise and walk.

The ogress, too, by then was up, although weak from loss of blood. Her skin gleamed palely through the curls of light brown hair, looking all the lighter next to the Bretons, all of them black-haired, except for Acfrud.

They made their way up the stairs and into the great hall of the Castle of Worst Luck. A faint humming noise could be heard from outside, and when they got the doors open it turned into a buzz as busy as a hive of bees, but the business was spinning thread. The bag of stuff gathered from the mulberry trees had been emptied just inside the entrance.

Bradamant, remembering vaguely that silk was supposed to grow on trees, thought at first that she was looking at big mulberries being spun so busily on great wheels, and was puzzled that the big, smooth, dull-white fruit heaped by the workers looked nothing like the dark, thin, quilty-surfaced mulberries. Then she blinked and looked again, seeing how almost all the white "fruits" were burst open at one end. They were cocoons, and she remembered the cloud of white-wings that had cloaked the ogress.

Not quite all of the cocoons had hatched. A few were unbroken, and one of the castle spinsters had a half a dozen of these soaking in a pot of water, over a small fire. She had teased an end off each of the half dozen, loosened by the moist heat, and these, twisted together, she was reeling onto a separate wheel, yards and yards of it, rolling out as if the cocoons could never come to an end. The threads running from the cocoons to the twist were so fine that Bradamant could not see them, and even the six-fold thread of the twist was so thin that it was hard to see, and yet it never broke as the spinster pulled it round the wheel. The skein gathering there gleamed wherever light glanced from it, even brighter than the skeins the others were spinning from the broken cocoons.

The spinsters glanced uneasily at their wounded mistress. They were too absorbed by the work to look up directly, but they were uneasy at the incursion. They were clad in fine silks.

They did not seem to think that they were in need of rescue.

Mulberry gave a grunt, and they relaxed again into the hum of the wheels singing in the hall. Light glittered at each turn of the wheels, scattered by the growing mass of silken thread going around.

Mulberry went on past the spinsters into the great hall. Here there were several work-tables, with benches, and she sat down at one, making a sign to Duoda, who set off, her silk reeds rustling about her, on some errand. Bradamant guessed that it was a fresh robe for the ogress, although she hoped food for guests might be part of it.

They seemed to be guests, by now.

Beyond the work-tables were looms of oak, one of them immense, reaching up to the ceiling of the great hall. Bradamant was not surprised to see them. Nominoe had said in the first place that the maidens of the Castle of Worst Luck had been kept in King Arthur's time to make silk, a secret skill known nowhere else in Europe. Rather, Bradamant was surprised at what she did not see on the largest of the looms. Any respectable maiden's education included spinning, weaving, and sewing, and Bradamant knew just how complicated a task it was to weave patterns directly into cloth, rather than embroidering them on afterwards. The task became easier—although still not simple—if the patterns were made up as much as possible of long straight lines going up-and-down or across. The horsetail-reeds pattern Duoda wore was made up of short bands of color piled in straight vertical lines. Bradamant could have done the same, on a loom with no more than four harnesses. But when the edges of a segment of color needed to slant and keep changing their slant to make the lobes of an autumn leaf, such as Acfrud wore, for instance, that was quite another matter.

It could be done by weaving to show off the cross-threads, using many shuttles, and counting off the threads to put the color on one shuttle through *here* and taking it as far as *there* on the one set of neutral-colored threads strung on the loom, and then continuing the line with another color on another shuttle, instead of tossing one shuttle the whole yard's width of the loom. Then the other set of neutral threads could be brought forward, and the same process of many shuttles repeated in reverse.

But weaving to show off the weft gave a nubbly effect, as the weft threads wove over and under the taut lines of the warp bound tightly on the loom. It didn't shine with the gloss of weaving to show off the long, straight lines of the warp, keeping most of the weft hidden at the back. To change the colors on the warp, you wanted someone sitting at the top of the loom to go through the pegs at each pass of the shuttle and pull up the particular threads—some three or four thousand of them—that you wanted brought forward, with so many of this color *here* and so many of that color *there*. It would take a quarter of an hour or so for a quick top-worker to pull up a set of threads for each pass of the shuttle. Working all day and every day for a couple of months would give you a piece of cloth about a yard square, and in less than a year you would have enough for a robe.

But there was no perch at the top of the loom for the lightest of the spinsters to sit up there counting off threads.

Instead there was—Bradamant started toward the loom for a closer look, pausing to glance at Mulberry in case the ogress objected to letting an outsider see it.

Mulberry made a sound like clearing her throat, and Arganthael said, "You may look."

At the top of the loom, the threads were splayed out over a bar and tied to hooks, making a row so wide it nearly filled the width of the hall. Behind the hooks was a long strip of some kind of heavy paper, just as wide, punched full of holes. Goggling, Bradamant saw that the holes in any given row snagged on to the corresponding hooks, to pull up the individual strings and release them when the paper was pulled up a notch. Getting paper heavy enough to take the pull of the taut threads without tearing or sagging must be difficult. Making it was perhaps another of Mulberry's secrets. The work of figuring out where to punch the holes—not to mention punching them and doing it accurately—would be long and tedious. But once it was done, the pattern could be woven with hardly a pause between each throw of the shuttle. The cloth that would take months to weave could be done in half a day. Even allowing a day or two to rethread the loom and tie the hooks, it was amazing speed.

Bradamant looked back to see Mulberry and the whole troop of spinsters enjoying her astonishment. Nominoe, by contrast, was baffled, although paying close attention. But, then, his education had not included weaving.

Duoda returned briefly, carrying a clean robe for the ogress and a tray with a pitcher of water and cups. The robe was of the same pattern as before, but in different colors, with the berries in pale green, and brown for the branches. Acfrud gently helped the ogress out of the bloody silk and into the clean. Duoda went out again, continuing her errands.

Bradamant took a cup of water and sat down at the table across from Mulberry. Nominoe helped Marrec to do the same.

There was an awkward silence. Nominoe, who had intended to rescue maidens held in captivity, did not know what to say to the ruler of the castle which was so plainly not a prison at all. And Mulberry had no interest in smoothing his way by opening a conversation.

Bradamant, for something to say, looked at the spinsters, and at the one who was reeling together the unbroken fibers from the cocoons that hadn't hatched. "Wouldn't it be easier," she said, "if you harvested all the cocoons before they hatched?"

There was a murmur of suppressed agreement from the spinsters when Arganthael repeated this question in Breton, but the ogress did not even bother to tell her what answer to give. This was an old argument, long since settled by Mulberry. Arganthael answered in French, "The silkworms, my lady, would not come to our mistress's call, if they found that the most of them died without waking to spread their wings. The work we saved on spinning would go to hunting them in the wild, if we could find them at all, or keeping them closed indoors all their lives, if indeed we could learn how to keep them alive so. Without someone to call to them, I am sure it would be easier to herd them within-doors than to leave them free. But it is easier to leave them free, with Mulberry to call them—and she wants them to be free."

Nominoe said quietly, "But are you free?"

The ogress, much insulted, let out a growl so angry that Bradamant could not help wondering if it was true after all that ogres ate their enemies.

Duoda, luckily, reappeared just then, bringing a loaf of sliced bread and a bowl of honey. It was simple food, but it reminded them all that they were, at least for the moment, considered definitely as guests and, therefore, not enemies.

Mulberry, still looking angry, bit into a slice of bread. Her teeth were large, but not really much like tusks, when viewed without panic. She did not drool.

Arganthael took a breath to steady herself and told Nominoe, "We are free to go if we choose, my lord."

"But then—" Nominoe said. But the question was so obvious that he stopped short without finishing it.

Arganthael looked at him, and then at Acfrud, hesitating. Acfrud, although she put out a hand to touch Marrec's, was equally silent.

But Mulberry answered for them, and Arganthael, although reluctant to refuse Nominoe on her own, outright, translated for her.

Bradamant thought at first that Mulberry was speaking in some ogre-ish tongue of her own that she had taught the others, but realized after a little that Mulberry was speaking Breton to them. But she spoke deep in her throat, with no high-pitched ee-sounds, and Bradamant could see that even Nominoe had difficulty following what she said until Arganthael repeated it in French, and Marrec had trouble following either one.

Mulberry said, "Some want not to marry. Some want not to have children. Some want not to be under orders."

"Aren't they under your orders?" Bradamant asked.

"They are," Mulberry agreed, but added, "Not so many orders from me. They do not like my orders—they run away. No one follows. No one brings them back. Some fathers, mothers, husbands, rulers—some give many orders. They follow runaways."

"But there must be authority in any society, wherever they go," said Nominoe. "You admit to giving orders yourself. They can't run forever."

Arganthael answered for herself now. "Let's grant that, my lord. What you wanted wasn't an order, in my case, not exactly. But you want to rule more than just our village—you are hoping for all of Britanny. It will mean war, and living always among powerful people whose help you will need and whose enmity you will fear. A leader like that needs a wife who can rule while he's at war—and enjoy it. A wife who can help him manage his friends and rivals—and enjoy that, too."

"I think it may not need war," said Nominoe, with a glance at Bradamant. He thought a moment more and said, "If you did not want to take much part in dealing with those friends and rivals around us—I wouldn't force you to try."

Marrec and Acfrud, meanwhile, had been talking quietly together, in Breton, looking as unhappy as the other couple. Bradamant could not follow what they said, but Nominoe told her later that the dispute between them was in Acfrud's fear of childbirth. The men in Marrec's family had lost four wives in the year before—his uncle's, a brother's, and two cousins'.

Bradamant guessed that some of the others in Mulberry's Castle of Worst Luck had fears like those, some had fled from husbands who beat them, and some were lovers of women who wanted to avoid having a husband of any sort. The unmarried among them might have taken refuge in nunneries, easily enough, but, then, if they had changed their minds, they could not have left as easily as Mulberry claimed they could from her castle. It might have been different in the days when other ogres ruled the castle, but there did not seem to be anyone there now who wanted to return to the village with their rescuers.

Nominoe, however, had thought of another possibility. "But do you have to live here in hiding?" he asked. "You could visit—you could trade." In spite of his grief at Arganthael's refusal to go home with him, he could not help thinking like the head of a village. His eyes gleamed at the thought of the profits they could all make if the ogre started sending out woven silks to trade. "People would pay dearly for your fabrics."

"What does castle need?" Mulberry asked. "Soft-people goods," she added scornfully.

"But the looms—" said Bradamant, "—you must weave more than you need for just yourselves."

"Old ones," said Mulberry. This seemed to be intended as an explanation.

Arganthael added, "There are statues of their forebears in the castle. We weave robes for them. It's a way to show respect for the dead, I think."

"We always live here," said Mulberry. "Before the soft people come, we are here."

"But there must be things you would like to have if you traded," Nominoe argued. "More colors of dyes? Jewels to ornament the fabrics? Do you have enough salt? Spices?"

Mulberry did not seem to consider any of these worth an answer.

"Information about other ogres?" Bradamant suggested.

Mulberry stiffened, grimaced as the motion pulled on her injured side, and made herself relax. "None," she said.

"You can't be sure of that," said Bradamant. "If you send traders and tell them what to look for, or go with them yourself—there might be some to find."

"Where?" Mulberry demanded.

"The islands of the Mediterranean? There was one there somewhere until just a few years ago."

"Where now?"

"We think he died."

"Soft people killed."

"I think they did," Bradamant admitted. "But—"

Mulberry held up a hand for silence. Leaving the table, she went once round the spinning wheels, pausing occasionally to praise good work with a pat or to point out a thinness or swelling in the thickness of the thread to correct. She looked back at Bradamant thoughtfully, then left the hall.

Their audience was over.

Arganthael and Acfrud walked with them as far as the end of the mulberry grove. Marrec and Acfrud continued their discussion, without coming to any solution, although once he said something that startled her a good deal. But after the first gasp of surprise, she went back to looking discouraged.

Bradamant looked inquiringly at Nominoe, who explained the disagreement to her, and said that Marrec had been suggesting that he and Acfrud might live together without having children. This was a concession Acfrud had not thought he would make. But there were practical difficulties to not having children, and she did not want to trust her life to the reliability of decoctions of pennyroyal, or the like.

Bradamant wondered if their priest would approve of such an arrangement. When she asked, Arganthael gave a shrug. Nominoe commented, looking sideways at her, "If they try it, and if they decide to ask his opinion, and if they can't accept his ruling, she could always come back here."

"Could she, indeed?" said Arganthael, with an angry sidelong glance at Bradamant.

Nominoe held out his hands in a gesture of puzzlement.

Arganthael spoke to Bradamant. "You could not get rid of Mulberry with the sword, my lady, but you found another way. I think in the end she will go south to the sea to look for other ogres."

"That may be," said Bradamant, "but why should that prevent your sisterhood here from going on?"

"Without the mistress to guard against attacks?"

"Why not?" said Bradamant. "Trade the silks and hire guards."

"And without the mistress to call the silk-caterpillars? I don't think we could farm them on our own."

"It doesn't have to be silk," Bradamant pointed out. "Trade for wool or linen and weave your patterns that way."

"Not linen," said Arganthael, "It's hard to get it to take a dye. But wool—" She was lost for a moment in calculations.

Nominoe smiled a little, looking at her. Then he said, half joking and half in hope, "Then you would be the new mistress there at the castle, my lady, or so it seems to me. If you want to avoid the troubles of ruling and rivals, this may not be the best way."

Arganthael pleated a fold of silk between her fingers, pulling against its strength. "I think you would do better to look elsewhere, my lord," she said, after a little.

"But you can't stop me from waiting for you, if I choose."

"I cannot."

"You could try. You could tell me there is no hope for me in waiting," he suggested.

She was silent.

They had reached the edge of the mulberry grove. The lovers kissed, Arganthael and Nominoe holding tightly to each other, for a long moment, Acfrud and Marrec more gently, because of his injured shoulder. Then Arganthael and Acfrud slipped free and turned back to the Castle of Worst Luck.

Nominoe said wryly to Bradamant, "I think you have done me a favor, my lady, but I could not swear to it."

"Send me word, my lord, when you have decided," she said.

They made their way into the forest.

Chapter 8
The Horn's Voice

Bradamant asked at the tumble-down bishop's house for Leidrad, but the old monk who answered told her the bishop was not there.

"Out of town?" said Bradamant, surprised.

"No, no, no," said the old man impatiently. "Up the hill." West of the Saone the land rose up, and crested with the hill of the Fourvières.

"Oh," said Bradamant. "Of course. Festival night." It was the beginning of harvest-time. She could ask the old man to arrange her lodging with the nuns of St. Peter and wait to ask Leidrad's advice in the morning, but she had been sitting still on the hippogriff's back a long time, and walking into Lyon from the meadow where she had left the hippogriff had not stretched her much. A trudge up the hill of the Fourvières would help her sleep.

She turned away from the river, its current almost invisible in the gathering shadow, and set out toward the Fourvières. She was glad of her helmet in case any loose tiles fell. The cathedral of St. Etienne and the church of St. John beside it needed repairs as badly as the bishop's house, although he was evidently going to leave his own dwelling until last. Charlemagne had sent his old friend, Leidrad of Bavaria, into Lyon to rebuild, and encourage traders, and set up schools, as well as administering the see. It was an old city, and there was much to do. Its history went back to the Roman Empire—the Emperor Claude had been born there.

Climbing the hill, she came out of the lowland darkness into the last light of the day. Across the two rivers, the Saone and the Rhone, the setting sun was easing into a layer of bright pink clouds.

She reached the top just as the bonfires were being lit, and spotted the bishop, wrapped in his cloak, sitting on a stool beside the first fire, and eating a piece of whortleberry pie. He no longer needed the help of a razor to keep his hair in a tonsure.

She took off her helmet for easier recognition, and joined him. He waved hospitably to her to take a seat on the ground beside him, and nodded to one of his attendants. The youngster cut her a slice of pie and poured a bowl of wine.

Footraces were already beginning among the young folks, and some were daring each other to make the leap over the bonfires. It was the eve of St. Peter in Bondage.

"What brings you to Lyon?" said the bishop. "I haven't seen you since we settled who had to repave how much of the road to Marseille."

"How is the road holding up?"

"So-so. Perhaps I can talk the new governor into having Marseille do most of it next time."

"Perhaps I should warn him that you drive a hard bargain."

"He knows." The bishop gave her his sweetest smile.

Bradamant took a mouthful of pie, and licked her hand after she wiped her chin clean. It was juicy, and too good to waste. "I've come to look for a voice."

The bishop raised his eyebrows. "What do voices look like?"

She held out Astolf's silent horn. "Like that, when it's at home."

He ran his hand along the smooth graining of the dark curve, and touched the silver that bound it at the bell and the tip. It was as big as a wild-ox horn, and heavy. "Lyon's badge is a horn," said Leidrad, musing. "A horn-of-plenty, for its abundance." Leidrad put it to his lips, glanced at her for permission, then tried blowing into it. The veins in his forehead swelled, and his cheeks grew red, but no sound came out. The horn had no voice.

Bradamant put her hand to his shoulder. He was stubborn enough, perhaps, to keep on trying all night, or until a stroke stopped him.

He gave it back to her and was still a few moments, to let the air he could not force into the horn come out of his chest, and to draw fresh air in. He sat panting, then rubbed at his temples. "What makes you think its voice is in Lyon?"

"When my cousin Astolf came back from the Moon, the horn lost its voice somewhere in the wind. It was dumb when he landed in Marseille. When he looked in a vision, he saw Lyon spread out beneath him."

Leidrad frowned a little at her reference to Astolf's wonder-working. "Is it worth so much trouble?" he asked.

"Sometimes. It strikes panic into anyone in earshot."

"Indeed?" The bishop turned the horn, watching the reflections of firelight scatter along the surface. "Useful in battle, then. No army could stand up to it."

Bradamant looked at him sharply. "You aren't thinking—"

He laughed. "Why not? What does Duke Astolf mean to do with it? I could suggest some plans to him."

"Nothing," said Bradamant earnestly.

He looked at her in some surprise.

"It isn't his."

His surprise turned to astonishment.

It took Bradamant a moment to understand his confusion. "Oh, it's not stolen," she said.

"I am relieved to hear it," he said dryly. "But—?"

"The fairies gave it to him. They want it back."

For a moment, the bishop looked almost as shocked as if she had, after all, accused her cousin of being a thief. But he held silence, considering the matter. "Before the Saracens' invasion," he said at last, "I would have said that was trafficking with devils." He looked down at her abruptly. "Did you want to go to confession while you're here?"

"Yes, thank you. But I don't plan to confess to trafficking with devils. I haven't."

"Trafficking with the fairies?"

"If you tell me it's a sin and I should confess it, I suppose I will." She sipped at her bowl of wine. It was Beaujolais, made in the bishop's own fields. It was sweet and smelled of the summer warmth. "But I'm not sure what I can do to repent if it's a sin—at least, not while I'm looking for their own goods to give them. If I gave up the quest, I'd have the sin of breaking my word on my conscience, and it would be thieving of a sort, too. The things they're asking us to return came from them in the first place. If the ones who accepted the gifts were sinning, can it be a sin to give them back?"

He nodded absently, without arguing the point.

Bradamant, suddenly annoyed with him, said, "After all, you're easy enough on Bishop Felix, and he—"

"Oh, child!" Leidrad's face showed a complicated mixture of defiance, amusement, exasperation, and reproach. "Felix of Urgel is a saint! Everyone who's met him realizes that."

"A saint?" That was a wild claim to make for someone living.

Leidrad made a smoothing gesture with his hands, acknowledging that he had gone too far. "I don't say that he works miracles. But he's good-hearted, and generous, and just being around him makes you feel more hopeful of —" He stopped and thought a moment. "I don't know that there are many saints who've had so sweet a temper. Saints have to be sterner."

"He's been convicted as a heretic for Adoptionism," said Bradamant, going on the attack. Bishop Felix had, indeed, been convicted several times of the heresy of thinking that Jesus was God's adopted son. He kept recanting, but when he wasn't up on trial for it, he couldn't seem to stop himself from thinking what he thought, and, what was worse, saying it.

"He's kept as a prisoner in my custody," said Leidrad defensively.

"You treat him like a guest."

Leidrad looked hurt. He disapproved of heresy—but he had no intention of proving it at the cost of executing Felix. It was inconsistent, but he was not a saint with a saint's sternness, either. He knew several good arguments to settle Bradamant's doubts about breaking a promise and leaving Felix of Urgel alone, but the combination was unsettling. Either of the two sets of arguments seemed to weaken the other. He let both points go and remained silent.

Bradamant, however, still wanted to know if he thought she was dealing with devils. "Before the invasion—?" she prompted.

He folded his hands and returned her look. "Before the fighting, I would have said that the fairies were clearly demons. But their gifts did much to save us in that war. Great good could be done with such gifts. With your magic horn, we could carry invasion into the Saracens' lands."

"We could," said Bradamant, "but the king has as much as he can do to hold the empire together as it is."

"We could win the cities of Jerusalem and Bethlehem, and not have to depend on the Caliph's whims when the pious wanted to go there on pilgrimage."

"I'd rather worry about the Caliph's whims than have all the guides and innkeepers along the way angry at us for bringing a war their way."

"That wouldn't last long—pilgrims pay."

"Perhaps you're right," said Bradamant.

Leidrad looked at her quizzically, but did not press her further, except to say, "I hope you'll talk to me again before you give it away." He wrapped his cloak more tightly around him, and gave a little shrug. "It is difficult to know what to think of these spirits of air and fire, even with the clearest teachings of the Church to guide us. These fairies and heathen gods with their marvels are all devils in disguise, some say, but the Church does not condemn them all. Some are transformed wonderfully into saints, and their marvels baptized." He looked into the flames as two youngsters came bursting over, and staggered as they landed, catching at each other's hands, then whooped and ran on by. "St. Peter in Bondage—Lammastide, Duke Astolf would call it? To bless the first loaves and the start of harvest-time."

"Yes."

"They have been celebrating that feast a long time on top of the Fourvières in Lyon. Before it was the saint's feast, it was the feast of Rome and the Emperor Augustus, and before that it was the festival of Lugos, the shining raven-spirit who gave his name to Lyon. The name of the feast has changed, but it's still the same."

"No, it isn't," she couldn't help objecting. "It's in honor of God."

Leidrad took another bite of pie. "Now it is transfigured. But I think being grateful for the harvest must always have been pleasing to God, even before they knew whom to thank."

The young attendant, looking mischievous, began to sing a song about St. Peter—how he fell in love with a mortal woman and went early one Sunday to take a kiss from her lips.

Someone passed him a lute, and he cradled it, playing as he sang.

From beyond the fire, a woman sang the answering verse, how Peter's mistress turned into a doe running over the fields to leave him behind, but he turned into a hunter, and she to a carp, and he to an angler, and so on until he was Peter in Paradise, and she a star in the sky, and the lovers were together.

"So, Michel, that's your notion of St. Peter in Bondage, is it?" said Leidrad.

Michel smiled, without answering, and began to play variations of the tune, each one more intricate than the one before it. He had fine, straight hair that must have been fair when he was little. Now it was brown, but flecked with gold in the firelight. He was evidently a layman, and wore no tonsure.

Leidrad listened awhile, then turned back to Bradamant. "How much magic has your cousin sent with you? I can imagine you chasing a voice in the wind easily enough, but I don't see how you can hope to see it to follow it, or jump high enough to catch it if you do."

Bradamant shook her head. "Astolf didn't think he could locate it very closely, and even if we could, it could still blow away somewhere else when I went there. But to reach it if I can find it—I've borrowed Astolf's hippogriff."

Leidrad nodded, apparently willing to believe that there was nothing inherently sinful in a hippogriff. "But what about finding it, when you can't see it?"

Bradamant and Astolf had argued this question at some length. He thought it was pointless for her to make the attempt until he could find a spell that would let him spot its location exactly, instead of showing him only the general area. But even with his beautifully indexed book of magic spells back in his hands, he had not been able to improve his clear-seeing. Bradamant thought she might as well be up and doing—and the hippogriff enjoyed exercise—so here she was. "A horn isn't much of a net," she said, "but I thought I could at least try holding it out against the wind. You never know. Something might fall in."

Michel looked up from his lute. "You should try calling to it, Lady," he said.

"Calling?"

He broke off the chord he had begun, set his fingers carefully down on the strings, and plucked one. The others gave out the same note, although he had not touched them. One by one, he touched them into silence. "If you make the sound it plays—"

"I don't know what it sounds like."

"Oh." Michel set a finger on the second string, then plucked a note on the lowest string and damped it. The string beside it sounded, an octave higher. Then he put his finger further up and made a tone sound midway up the next octave. He kept going, the notes sounding fainter and farther away as they gave voice higher and higher above the base, calling one another up a distant scale. He stopped, and Bradamant became suddenly aware again of the voices around them. Heavy thwacks and cheers beyond the fire showed that stave-fighting had begun. Michel held out a hand. "May I see?"

Bradamant gave him the horn. He measured its length against his forearm. It was nearly twice as long. Then he peered inside, running his hand into it to feel the shape. "I don't know what difference magic makes, lady," he said, "but I think some hunting horns would sound the right notes."

Bradamant nodded slowly. It didn't sound hopeful, but it would be better than flying at it completely blind.

"See to it," said Leidrad. Michel nodded, and went back to playing.

As the fires grew low, people started gathering up their belongings and making ready to follow the path down the hill into town again.

"Time to be going," said Leidrad.

Bradamant yawned, and stretched out her arms and legs. She promptly regretted it, and pulled her knees up. She put her hands around her left calf, trying to hold in the sudden pain there.

"What—?" said Leidrad.

"Nothing, just a cramp in my leg."

"I could rub the muscle, Lady," Michel offered.

"No, it isn't a muscle."

Michel looked confused.

She wouldn't be able to get up for a few minutes, anyway. She began to explain. "It does that sometimes. I asked the king's councillor Isaac about it, a few years back, when it first started happening."

"It happens often?" said Leidrad.

"No, once a year or so. Isaac says it's a thickening of the blood, closing off the line of the vein. After a while fresh blood usually works its way through and opens it up again over the next few days. It comes from too much heaviness, when the heavy humor, phlegm, is drawn into the body over the years.

Air comes down the nose and throat and into the lungs, and if the phlegm comes, too, then it backs into the veins when the air is distilled into the arteries—if Aristotle is right in saying air travels in the arteries, that is."

"If?" said Leidrad. She had shocked him again. He had not read much of Aristotle himself, to be sure. Alcuin of York had brought a copy, in Latin, of the Ten Categories of Language with him to France, and that was all Leidrad was likely to get at. Greek books were rare, and impossible to come by, unless you visited the King of Greece in Byzantium, or traveled among the Saracens, as Isaac had done, and could read the translations they had made into their own tongues of the ancient treasures. But he knew Aristotle was an Authority—ancient, and immensely wise, and tested by time. And he knew Aristotle said somewhere that the arteries carried air to cool the body, to balance the hot blood that went back and forth in the veins. Dealing with fairies was one thing, but questioning Aristotle was another.

"Well, if you cut an artery, there isn't a rush of air. You get a spurt of blood, and you get it right away—and even if the air is too distilled to be felt, how can the vacuum suck blood out of the veins into the arteries down to the wound that fast?"

"All very well, but what would be the point of having *two* sets of vessels ebbing and flowing with blood in your body?" said Leidrad tartly. "It isn't as if those precious physicians Isaac studies can find any connections to link veins to arteries. Two systems, two functions. That's logic. Besides," he added triumphantly, "if the heart isn't pumping air through the body, how can you get the surplus phlegm drawn in?"

"I don't know," said Bradamant. "Isaac says the physicians like to argue it."

"Physicians like to argue," said Leidrad.

The pain had started to ease up. She could not put much weight on the leg, but Michel and another of the bishop's attendants helped her. Leidrad took a torch, and they followed him down the hill.

The next day, after making her confession, Bradamant waited outside the cathedral for Michel to turn up with a hunting horn for her to borrow. She leaned against the wall under a panel of old limestone, finely carved down the middle, although much worn. She wondered if it would last through the re-building. It showed a woman, looking out thoughtfully with wide, staring eyes. Fruit and flowers overflowed on her breast from the mouth of a long, narrow horn-of-plenty she held in her arms. Saint Dorothy, Bradamant thought vaguely, then thought it ought to be a gardener's basket in that case. A figure of Lyon itself? She wondered if the magic that put plenty in a horn was at all like the magic to put in terror, or if they were as different as their effects. Perhaps Astolf would know.

Michel arrived in a few minutes, looking pleased with his success, and handed over a brass horn. "Couldn't find one of horn that sounded likely, but I think this will be right, Lady." The phrasing was cautious, but his look was confident, and she thanked him warmly.

He packed it away for her in a leather sheath and helped her fasten it by its strap over her shoulder. She already had the magic horn on the other shoulder, her sword at her belt, and two pouches, one carrying her bit of fairy gold and other oddments of her own, and the other heavy with oats to give the hippogriff a treat, as well as a long scarf about her neck, and her helmet and mail on. It made an awkward load—not heavy, but it hemmed her in, and the day promised to be hot. Still, the walk out of town to rejoin the hippogriff would not take her long, and once in the wind it would be cool enough.

She thanked Michel again. He gave her his engaging, mischievous smile, and bowed to her, as she strode away, still limping slightly on the phlegmatic leg. He leaned beside the stone lady and watched her out of sight.

The hippogriff could fold his horse legs to sleep lying down. But he liked it better if there was a perch just high enough off the ground for him to perch with his lion legs folded and the eagle head tucked under one wing, his body supported comfortably, and his horse legs standing on the ground, knees locked.

He had found a tree with a suitable crotch at the edge of the meadow, where a little grove began. He was whistling gently in his sleep, a sort of hippogriff snoring, as Bradamant returned to the meadow.

At her approach, his head went up, and he stepped forward on his hooves, pulling his lion hindquarters free of the perch to the ground, ready to rear and fight or take off and fly. At sight of Bradamant, he gave a snort, and shook himself, settling his hair and feathers comfortably, and trotted forward at a gentle pace to meet her. He was good at foraging for himself, but gave a small scream of approval at the oats. He nosed suspiciously at the handful of berries she had thrown in, for the holiday, then sniffed, and pecked them up.

As they rose into the sun, Bradamant could see the horse races going on to the east, in the low ground beyond both the rivers, where the city was not built so densely as it was on the peninsula between the rivers and along the Saone's western bank. On the Rhone, beside the race-course, the boatmen were doing good trade, with passengers who wanted to cross, or to lounge along the river for the day.

Faintly, she could hear people cheering the riders. From so high above, it sounded like a murmur. If she had had Marron there, he would have enjoyed showing off his strength for the crowd. And no doubt he would have won, and she would have enjoyed that. Then again, it would hardly have been a fair contest. The hippogriff was not so old a friend as her horse, but, all the same, it was exhilarating to rise in the air with him, watching the trees grow small while the land spread out before her, as if blown into being by the wind of their flight.

The hippogriff found a draft of air rising up and opened his wings, gliding in a circle that kept them hovering, effortless, in the sky.

When she judged they were high enough not to spook the horses, Bradamant set about blowing her borrowed horn, sending out notes in all directions, trying a different pitch as she completed each round of the spiral.

She heard nothing.

A pair of ravens speeding by below came into the rising wind and glided up to meet them, looking fierce. Their head feathers were ruffled, twitching at the sides into tips like tiny horns. The hippogriff screamed at them, and they smoothed down. They beat their wings gently and settled one on each side of the hippogriff, each with one eye gazing directly into one of the hippogriff's eyes. The hippogriff, his view restricted to little more than a pair of bright raven eyes filling the world, bore with them patiently. At last he snorted, and dropped down a little, freeing his vision.

The ravens flew on a little further, now eye to eye with each other.

The hippogriff gave a grunt.

The ravens flew out of the draft, and the hippogriff followed. Bradamant started to call to him to stop, but then decided she might as well trust to the hippogriff's hunch. She had not tried all the possible combinations of tone and direction, but if the hippogriff thought it was time to try casting over another part of the sky, there was no harm trying. Maybe his ears could hear more than a human did—or maybe the ravens' could.

The ravens found another draft a few miles away, but when the hippogriff joined them, they darted off again. They rejected yet another draft in the same way, but the next time the hippogriff joined them, they all hovered peacefully together in the wind, the ravens rising a little higher than the hippogriff, one to each side, eyeing Bradamant.

Bradamant sounded the horn. An echo answered, a low, quiet tone, that seemed to enter into the blood and build there, squeezing everything inside her.

The hippogriff screamed and bolted, veering off to the side and away. The ravens scattered, too, and Bradamant was too frightened to try to quiet the hippogriff at first.

When the hippogriff's pace slowed, and her own panic subsided, she told the hippogriff, "Now let's try something." She bound the scarf she had brought with her around the hippogriff's head, covering his ears tightly, then headed back in the direction the echo came from. After a little, she tried blowing the horn again. The sound was still ahead of her, but by the time she had recovered her wits enough to try again, it was behind her. She chased it back and forth, losing it now and again as a gust of wind flung it away, but each time finding the trace again, and following it more closely.

Suddenly, she felt the magic horn tremble at her side, and when she blew the borrowed horn again, it was the magic horn itself that answered.

Bradamant clutched at the hippogriff's mane. It took her some moments to realize that she didn't need to. Her heart was pounding in expectation of terror, but she was not terrified. She held the horn, and the horn held its own voice, and its spell was cast outward.

She took the scarf off him, and guided the hippogriff back to the grove by the meadow where she had left him before. There was a stream nearby, and she gave him a steadying hand on the rump while he bobbed his head up and down into the stream for a good long drink, then left him to his perch and a nap. She made her way back into town. Her leg had stopped hurting, and she was no longer limping.

Lyon was deserted, for most of the townsfolk were still beyond the Rhone to watch the races and games, and enjoy their holiday before the main work of the harvesting began.

She walked along, whistling tunelessly, and was a good deal surprised when two men in leather jackets and helms, with leather shields, bounced out from a doorway as she turned into the cathedral square. They raced at her, swords ready.

Bradamant stopped and sounded the magic horn.

They kept coming, deaf to its magic.

She swung at one with the borrowed brass horn, knocking him against the other, and gained a moment's respite to draw her own sword.

The one she had hit let out a squawk of pain and outrage. She had expected him to be hurt, but the note of protest made her take a moment more to peer at as much of his jaw as she could see beneath the helm.

It was Michel.

Bradamant grunted with exasperation and circled in on them, keeping them from getting on opposite sides of her.

She had no shield, but she used the brass horn as a stave in her left hand. It was going to be ruined. She could see that the prospect daunted Michel, although it did not seem to have occurred to his friend. Michel kept trying to attack straight to her sword arm, to avoid putting in a blow on the brass.

Bradamant waited for his excitement and anxiety to make him careless of keeping his shield well in place before him. He let the shield drift off to his side, leaving his front exposed as he tried to strike at her. She knocked the blow aside and drove in at him, bringing the sword down on his side.

Or she meant to. Her weak leg gave way, and her sword cut into his leg.

His sword caught on the side of her head as she fell. The strap of her helmet gave way, and it came off. Her long hair tumbled loose.

Her head was ringing with the blow, and she could feel that her leg would give out again if she put her full weight on it.

She let herself drop and rolled, fetching up against the wall. She braced herself against it and scrabbled up, then swung her sword high, ready to cut down on the first to strike. She stood panting, trying to focus her eyes.

Nothing seemed to be happening.

"—two to one, says you. Grab it and get out, says you," said an infuriated voice. "Didn't say One of the king's champions, did you? Hold still, damn you!"

The speaker had taken off Michel's helm and his own and edged the plugs of wax out of their ears. He was taller and heavier, but the fine straight hair, and something in the line of the cheeks, identified him as a kinsman, no doubt Michel's brother. Michel was on the ground, his leg bleeding freely as he struggled to get up. His brother glanced at Bradamant's sword. "Lady, I yield," he said quietly. "So's he, as soon as I can make him. Can I have that?"

Bradamant was puzzled, thinking he must mean the magic horn, and thinking that they had already settled that question. She gripped it more tightly.

"No, *that*," he said, annoyed with her slowness. He jerked his head at it.

"Oh!" said Bradamant. He was after the scarf. She tugged it free from her neck and dropped it. He wound it in and set about binding it around Michel's leg.

"But, Claude—" Michel protested.

"Hold still!" Claude repeated.

"But is it all right?"

"Will be. Good thing it wasn't your hand."

"No, I mean—"

Bradamant, realizing what he meant, set the brass horn down where he could reach it. "Can it be fixed?"

Michel looked it over with disgust. "I don't think so. Maybe the bishop will forgive me the cost."

"I should think he would," said Bradamant, dryly.

"This wasn't his idea!" Michel cried, catching the intended accusation.

"No?"

"It wasn't!"

He was younger than she had realized, to be so irritated at having his word doubted by a stranger, who had no way to know if his word was necessarily good.

"You mean he didn't tell you to do it," said Bradamant, softening her judgment both of Michel and of Leidrad. "But you had his thoughts in your mind. You wouldn't have hit on it for your own amusement." She leaned against the wall and caught a smell of berry tart. There was a bakery inside, it seemed, with festival pie to offer. "He isn't going to be pleased with you."

"You have to tell him," said Claude, not quite making it a question.

Bradamant hesitated.

"Doesn't matter," said Michel. "Think we could both go through confession more than once without one or other of us letting it out?"

"Probably you," said Claude, scowling. "We'll have to go away. Charlotte isn't going to like this."

"Your wife?" said Bradamant.

Claude shook his head, glancing down at his brother.

"You heard her," said Michel. "She likes to sing. But we're not—I couldn't ask her to leave Lyon."

"Why not?" said Claude and Bradamant in unison, and looked at each other in surprise. Claude shrugged. "No harm asking." He took Michel's arm over his shoulders, hoisted him up, and started a retreat into the bakery. Michel tenderly caught the damaged brass horn up into his arms.

"Go to Paris," said Bradamant. "Tell Lady Alda I...recommend your loyalty as servants." She turned away to cut their thanks short. She was not in a mood to accept any.

She plodded away, limping a little again, toward the cathedral. She thought the woman holding Lyon's horn-of-plenty in the stone must be old enough to satisfy Oberon's liking. She started toward it, but before she could get there, she heard wings beating. Before she could look around to see what was happening, the sound stopped, and she staggered with the sudden weight.

She had a raven on each shoulder. Even through her mail she could feel the pressure of the talons clutching at her to keep the ravens balanced.

"Hey!" she said. One of the ravens was tugging at the strap that held the magic horn. Even if she was right in thinking that the stone horn up ahead would echo into fairyland, she could not make any progress toward it with this magpie-minded pair thieving at her shoulders.

She pulled the gold oakleaf out of her pouch and let it flash in her hand.

The raven not in reach of the shoulderstrap was intrigued and bent down to try to snatch the gleaming toy.

Bradamant closed her hand on the leaf and crossed her arms over her face, protecting her eyes, and frustrating the raven trying to pull the strap down from her shoulder.

Both ravens set up a squawking, as if calling for help.

It seemed like a good idea. "Oberon!" said Bradamant. "Claude!" she added, for good measure. He might be a doubtful sort of ally, but at least he was within human hearing.

The street ahead of her seemed very bright.

Behind her, she heard Oberon's voice. "It's all right," he said. "The ravens know where it goes."

She spun around, but there was no one there.

The raven pulling at the strap got it off her shoulder, at last, and gave a croak of gloomy satisfaction. Both ravens hopped to the ground.

Her shadow, stretching back toward the bakery, was dark and unreasonably tall.

Claude came running out, but staggered, throwing his hands over his face to protect his eyes. She looked around, and had to cover her own eyes. Even with eyes closed and hands over them, she saw gold brightness. She felt hot.

Then the golden warmth was gone. She opened her eyes, and the street up to the cathedral was empty.

"Who was that? Why did you give it to him, Lady?" Claude was standing beside her, blinking, and rubbing at his eyes.

"What did you see?" Bradamant asked him.

He stopped blinking, to stare at her in surprise, but seeing she wanted to know, he answered, "That man with the wide eyes. Just stretched his arms out and took the horn. Then the ravens gave a jump and settled in on his shoulders, and he—" Claude hesitated, as it occurred to him what an odd story he was telling. "He went to the stone with Dame Fortune on it, there, and on through into the church." He nodded at the figure of the woman with the horn-of-plenty.

They looked at the stone horn, and at each other, and trotted down the street to the old figure Claude spoke of as Dame Fortune. She looked just the same, and so did her cornucopia, but when Claude stretched out his hand to touch it, he grunted, pulled his hand back, and put his fingers in his mouth.

Bradamant put out her hand more cautiously. The cornucopia was hot.

They looked in the church door. There was no one inside.

Claude shrugged.

They started back to the bakery.

One of the ravens landed on the cornucopia, stretching itself as if nestling into a comfortable warmth, and settled down to preen itself. Its mate was not in sight, but they heard one croaking call, from the sky above the cathedral.

"It looks as if Leidrad has the horn after all," said Bradamant, nodding at the cornucopia.

"Or Dame Fortune does," said Claude. He made a tsking noise. "Bring luck to the building he's doing."

Bradamant nodded thoughtfully. "I'm sorry it turned out ill luck for you and Michel."

Claude shrugged again. "Hasn't finished turning out yet." He looked back, staring over his shoulder at Dame Fortune. "Going to seek our fortune," he said. "You never know."

At the bakery door, he bowed and went inside, letting out a little breeze of pie smells, strong and hot.

Bradamant rubbed her mouth. She was too tired to be hungry. She thought she would take a little nap herself before she woke the hippogriff. Slowly, she headed down the sunny road, making her way back to the meadow.

Chapter 9
Malgis's Book

When she had crossed the Belgian lands before, in early spring, her cousin Malgis had been away from the Ardennes, hunting in other parts of the empire for herbs and simples. Now summer was almost over. He should have been back long since. Even so, he might be hard to find, for he knew all the caves in the forest, and lived in most of them, one time or another, when he rebelled against the king, supported by her brother.

But his main hideaway had been the caves a little south of Liège, on the swift-flowing Ourthes. He had built a tower rising over one of them, and pulled it down again, when he and Charlemagne finally patched up their quarrel. But the grotto underneath was still there, and gave protection against the weather. The forest was cold in winter.

She asked after him at an inn, while she bought bread and cheese and a skin of wine-and-water.

"The night-wizard?" said the old inn-woman. "Yes, I've seen him about—buys himself a little thread, and salt, and such-like. If you're buying a little favor, you could pay him in food, if—" She looked up from the sock she was knitting, to take the measure of Bradamant's sword and chainmail, and fell silent. This was not a customer paying in barter. She looked again, gauging Bradamant's expression. "You won't find him out by day like this, my lady. Nor not at all, if you might be meaning harm—meaning no harm to tell you so."

"I don't mean him any harm," said Bradamant patiently.

"He runs with the night goblins, the nutons, they do say," the inn-woman went on. She considered the armor again. "But you can take care of yourself, I suppose." She fell silent, worrying over the turn of the heel, to all appearances.

Bradamant thanked her and took the road into the forest. She left the hippogriff at the edge of the woods to rest and amuse himself—"Quietly!" she said, and thought he understood—while she was gone.

Malgis' cave was too well hidden, under the dark green leaves of the beech and chestnut and willow trees of the Ardennes, to find easily. On foot, though, she would have a better chance of spotting the marks of the trail than if she rode high in the air on a hippogriff, or even low, on horseback. As the road brought her into the shade of the glossy leaves, the air grew cool. She came at last to what she thought was the right track, although it was only a narrow way that could have been made by deer running in the woods. Still, it followed an outcropping of limestone cliffs, glinting grey through the ivy that grew up the sides, and Bradamant thought it was likely to be her way.

Malgis apparently wanted to discourage casual explorers, for there were stupid-stones in the grass—stumbling blocks to catch the unwary. At first she took them for ordinary stones, and threw them off the track each time one tripped her. At last she grew suspicious. She hid behind a tree and watched the stupid-stone roll merrily back onto the track. If she'd had a hammer along, and cared to go to the effort, she could have smashed them open to stop them. Perhaps it was just as well that she couldn't—Malgis would probably not appreciate it. As it was, she picked her way carefully and managed to avoid most of the stupid-stones. They caught her with only a few more spills.

When the track opened into a clearing wide enough to put her into sunlight, she thought perhaps she had reached the cave, but she could find no opening into the limestone, except one small cave that showed by the smell that it was a fox's den. Besides, she couldn't hear the Ourthes. She knew from her brother's accounts of the time he had spent there, in exile with Malgis, that the river was close by.

She found a grassy spot to sit down, and propped her feet up on a stone to ease them. Either it wasn't a stupid-stone, or it did not object to propping her, for it stayed where it was. Her feet ached from a longer walk than she had expected, and it was pleasant to sit quietly in the light. She brought out her food.

Then she heard metal chinking—like mail.

She recognized him this time. His shield was clear, or, rather, only dimmed a little by the dust of the road. The silver mountain glittered through the dirt. Bradamant set her cheese down neatly, on a beech-leaf, instead of dropping it and scrambling for her sword. She waved him a greeting and held out the wine-skin.

Her brother Renald's expression was mixed between pleasure and irritation at finding her there on the path before him.

Pleasure won, and he bent and kissed her. He sat down beside her, where the root of a chestnut tree pushed up above the level of the ground and made a convenient, if knobby stool.

Bradamant handed over a share of the bread and cheese.

He wriggled on the tree root, trying to find a comfortable spot, or the least uncomfortable spot. When he was settled, he shook his head, a little surprised at finding himself so hungry for bread and cheese, and took a large mouthful. "Going after Malgis's book?" he said, pausing from the cheese to reach for the wine. He took a swallow of it.

Bradamant nodded.

"Might have guessed," he said resignedly. "I'm in good health today, by the way."

"Well, I'll worry about that later," she said.

He nodded, and ate some more bread. "Forgot it was this far off the road," he said, when his mouth was clear. "Didn't want to risk Bayard's legs with the stupid-stones."

"He's all right?" said Bradamant, anxiously.

"Yes, I left him to forage by the road." Reminded, he took another bite.

Bradamant ran her finger down the tough, twiny length of a stalk of chicory. The chicory flowers were a bright, light blue, like bits of sky. They were just starting to close for the day, the sun being at its height. Chicory was a morning-lover. "What about you?" she said, after a little. "Come to tell him not to let me have it?"

Her brother shook his head slowly. The red in his hair had not quite all turned to brown. Streaks of coppery brightness caught the light. "Not exactly," he said.

"What—exactly?"

"I'm going to Cologne. I thought Malgis might like to go with me. You, too, if you've a mind to."

"Cologne," she said, feeling baffled. "An errand for the king?" It didn't seem likely to her, as she said it, and she knew it was wrong at the amusement that lit his face in seeing her unable to guess his riddle. With equal suddenness, the happy look vanished from his face, and his mouth turned wry. "I don't get along with Uncle, unless I stay out of his way. Never did. I don't see how you manage it."

"I keep my temper better," said Bradamant.

He started to contradict her, then realized he was proving her point, and said nothing. He took another swallow of wine. "They're building a cathedral in Cologne," he said then. "I thought I'd go help. Penance for sins—against Uncle, mostly."

Bradamant was startled. It was hard to imagine her brother summoning up the patience to haul bricks and mortar around. And what could he do with Bayard when he did it? Hitch him to a cart, and wear both of them out with the loading? It sounded like a heavy penance, taken all round.

"Doesn't sound like something to interest Malgis," she said, "unless you're thinking he could magic the walls into place."

"It's a cathedral!" Renald said.

"You wanted to use the magic helmet—"

"Not for that," he protested. "Maybe using it at all would have been wrong," he added, making a face. The muscles in his neck and shoulders tightened, and he looked away from her, down the path.

His eyes were not looking along the path, though.

Bradamant raised her eyebrows, and tried to guess where his gaze was going. "Is it much farther, do you think?" She looked idly down the track, setting her head at the same angle as his. Out of the corner of her eye, she scanned the beech trees there, looking for whatever it was that had put her brother so suddenly on the alert. There—that was it: a green shadow between two boles. Or was it another tree, slighter than its neighbors? the trunk of a willow showing between them, maybe? No, it was too human in its shape. But once she thought that, she thought also that it was too large, and too crookedly built, for a person. She tried to convince herself it must be a tree trunk, even if it did have a knob at the top like a face and bushy hair around it for leaves. The face of an ugly woman, she thought, with the skin dark and cracked, and eyes bulging like oak-galls. There was a weasel curled up against its feet, or its roots.

Not a tree. It moved. It crouched down, touched the weasel's head, then scrambled silently on all fours into the deeper shadows of the woods. There was no sound of leaf or twig.

Bradamant would have thought she'd imagined it, it was so quick and quiet in its vanishing, if Renald had not still been watching tautly beside her.

"What was that?"

"Woods giant. Giantess, maybe," said Renald. He shivered, and stretched himself, easing his muscles. "Used to be a many of them in the Ardennes."

"Are they dangerous?"

"They could be, I suppose. But Malgis had some kind of understanding with them, when we were hiding out here, and they never bothered us."

"Friendly, then?"

"I wouldn't go that far. Bad tempers, and more strength than is good for them." He stared into the darkness behind the trees again, but saw nothing. "We should be getting on."

Bradamant nodded at the chicory. It had finished closing up its flowers, and looked like a rack of dried twigs. "Present for our host?" she suggested.

"Its virtues aren't very powerful," said Renald. "Relaxes the bowels and encourages the water—good for jaundice and the ague."

"How are you feeling?" Bradamant said, wondering anxiously if his recollection of the last virtue was prompted by a need for it.

He smiled foxily, having misled her. "Well enough. Food and sleep are medicines, too. I wouldn't say no to a good salad, but otherwise I don't plan to ask Malgis for chicory, even if it is 'a fine, cleansing, jovial plant, take it how you will'." He was obviously quoting Malgis's expertise in the herbal.

Bradamant laughed. "All that, but not powerful?"

"If you take it in the light of Jupiter—" He stopped short. "Heathen magic," he said. His good humor had evaporated.

"Well, it's growing along the track. He must know it's here if he wanted it," said Bradamant practically, and set off along the faint path, stepping high to avoid a stupid-stone.

With Renald there, Bradamant stopped worrying about staying on the trail or locating the entrance to the cave. She concentrated on not stumbling and not getting snagged on low branches. After an hour or so, and only one fall each, they came to a halt. The trail ran close to the edge of a limestone cliff, most of its face hidden by thick ivy. There was no obvious break in the leaves, but they could hear water running somewhere nearby, and there were two piles of oddly assorted items heaped by the cliff—worn-out shoes, broken pots and pans, scraps of paper with messages in words or rough sketches, according to the sender's ability to write, and in the other mended goods and small leather bags or bottles filled with powder or potion. Renald looked doubtfully at a large chestnut growing a few paces farther along, then gave a little grunt and shook himself. "Grew taller," he murmured. He faced off from the tree, then led Bradamant straight into the face of the cliff—

—and through the ivy into the gloom of a limestone cave.

It was too dark to see, at first.

Renald put his hand to his sword. Bradamant could not see him do it, but she heard it in the sounds of leather and mail, and something in the way he breathed. Quietly, he drew it out of the sheath. She drew her sword, too, and they stood waiting for their eyes to grow used to the darkness.

There was a rustling noise, but it was moving back, away from them. "Who's there?" said Bradamant. There was no answer —frightened, or massing to jump at them?

Renald's eyes finished taking in the dim light first. "Nutons!" he said disgustedly, and although he kept the sword in his hand, his shoulders relaxed, with a faint clink of iron.

Now Bradamant could see them, too. They were as tall as ordinary people, but that was because of the domed hats they wore, rising high above their heads. Between the felt hat-brims and the tangled grey beards, there was not much to be seen of their faces. Here and there eyes caught a gleam of light, and vanished into shadow again, as the nutons shifted anxiously about, pulling away from the armed incursion. Even though they had the advantage of numbers, and their knives and hammers could have been formidable weapons, knives and hammers wielded by nutons did not have the reach of long swords held by long-limbed humans. And nutons were even shyer than other elves and goblins, belonging to the night as they did.

"We don't mean you any harm," said Renald.

"We're Malgis' cousins—we came to see him," said Bradamant.

The nutons milled about, catching each other's eyes, then pulled back together in a group, blocking the entrance to the inner caves. One of them edged forward, making slow, tiny steps even slower and tinier as he drew near the swords.

Bradamant sheathed her sword, and the nuton stopped where he was, watching Renald.

Renald stepped back and made the nuton a bow, but he came no closer.

"What do you want?" said Renald. He took a step forward, and the nuton skittered back among the others.

"Softer," said Bradamant. "They're frightened."

Renald glanced at the knives and hammers, and the number of nutons in the cave, and looked skeptically at his sister.

"Well, they are," she said.

The nuton made a squeaking noise, edged forward again, and stopped again.

Short of attacking the lot of them—which would present a considerable danger, and would not endear them to Malgis —there did not seem to be anything they could do. Renald waited a moment more, then laughed, and put his sword back in the sheath.

The nuton edged by them to the mouth of the cave, peered out into the daylight, squeaked again, and pulled back, rubbing his eyes. He turned and made an indignant shooing motion at them to get out of their cave at this unseasonable daylight hour, but there was a stir from the inner cave.

A nuton woman came out, and the others made way for her. Like the men, she wore tunic and trews and high felt cap, and there was not much difference between them, except that she was beardless. She was carrying a large wooden bowl in one arm and a wool blanket draped over the other. She handed the blanket to one of the men, who spread it over a heap of mosses off to the side, and nodded curtly to the pair of humans to be seated.

They accepted the hospitality, and sat.

The woman set the bowl between them. It turned out to be filled with salad, with a dressing of herbs. Another nuton, following behind her, gave them each a cup of beer. Then they were gone again, and the rest with them, although the humans had not seen them go, into the shadows of the inner caves.

Renald fingered the wool of the blanket. It was a good, dense weave. "Must be new," he said. "Moths get to them out here."

Bradamant looked at the darkness where the inner caves began. "Can't they talk?"

"I don't know. They never did to me." He sniffed suspiciously at the salad. His mouth twisted, and he fished a root out of the bowl, peered at it in the dimness, and showed it to Bradamant. It was chicory—not the wild chicory from the woods, but tame chicory, an endive root, with a sweeter, milder taste, and more meat to it.

"Better eating," said Bradamant, "even if it's not as 'jovial'." She took a swallow of the beer. It was sour, but as a matter of courtesy she drank it anyway. Besides, she was thirsty, and they'd used up most of the wine.

They talked quietly for a while. Renald told her how the crops were coming along at Montalban, and what the boys were up to. Bradamant told about Marfisa and Astolf. Renald had gone through Paris, and they compared notes on Alda's governing there.

It was still daylight outside when Malgis came rushing through the opening from the inner caves, rubbing the sleep-sand out of his eyes. His cousins scrambled to their feet to hug him.

The nuton woman stood for a moment in the mouth of the inner cave, eyeing them. But Malgis seemed to have no doubt that these were friends, not enemies, and she faded away.

Malgis was short and dark, unlike his cousins, taking after his mother's side. Being dark was convenient for him, in the caves. It made him hard to see. Renald and his brothers, when they had joined Malgis to build a stronghold there against the king's forces, had always had to be careful to hood themselves and muddy their faces, if they wanted to walk unseen. Secrecy came easily to Malgis. But Renald and Bradamant did not need to see the warmth of the grin on his face to know it was there as he said, as formally as if the grotto were a seigneury, "Welcome to my domain!"

"A domain, is it?" said Renald.

"My very own—well, yours, too, Cousin. Fair's fair."

"Kind of you, but I had my full share before." Renald lowered himself to the pallet of moss, and clucked his tongue, looking around at the bare, familiar walls. "It's hard on the bones, your domain. Winter especially." Bradamant sat down again with him.

"Yes, it's a good time to head south looking for rare herbs," said Malgis. "And even in summer—make room, can't you?"

Renald and Bradamant edged over, and Malgis settled himself between them.

For some time, they gossiped back and forth together, repeating all the family news.

But when Bradamant spoke of seeing Alda in Paris, Malgis said, "I went there, too, along toward spring's end. She mentioned she'd seen you." He waited expectantly for her to hear what he hadn't said.

After a moment, she caught it, and said, "You know why I'm here, then."

"Yes. But how does Renald come into it, I wonder? Not helping?"

Renald shook his head. "I was tired of exile, but I'm tired of being the king's good subject, too. I wanted something to do that—well—that matters."

"Come to study magic?"

Renald gave an irritable grunt, and went on. "A king's court comes to an end, in the end. So do magic spells, come to that."

"Do they?" Malgis looked at him closely. "Church, then. But you're old to take up holy vows, lad. Think they'll have you?"

"Not taking Orders."

"Well, then?"

"I'm going to Cologne. I'll help build the cathedral. That's a job that'll see my time out."

"I shouldn't wonder," said Malgis politely, and waited.

Renald gave him a sidelong look. The silence meant that Malgis had already turned down his invitation. But he said it anyway. "I want you to burn that demons' book and come with me."

"Not 'demons'." Bradamant muttered.

"'Demons' book'." said Malgis disgustedly. "'Fairies' book,' that's more your idea, I take it?" he added to Bradamant. He put his hand on Renald's shoulder and levered himself up from the pallet. He scowled at them, then stomped through the arch to the inner cave. In a few moments he was back, carrying his book of spells.

He had bound it in white leather, and indulged himself in extravagant decorations of tiny rubies, polished smooth, and fixed into the leather with silver wire, to form a border around the edges, and a high red mountain in the middle. With the book clasped in both arms, it was hard for him to sit down again between them, but after some stork-like stepping about to get himself poised just so, he plopped down again safely, with a grunt as the landing jarred his bones.

Renald touched the ruby that topped the mountain. "Could you go back to Aigremont? Surely the king would let you take up your estate—"

"He might," said Malgis. "But somehow I could never manage to work up the kind of interest you need in how the crops are doing, year in, year out, to do an estate justice. Wheat, for instance, such a tame sort of plant—"

"Tame!" both his cousins protested.

"There, now, you see? You take a proper interest. But it isn't like the herbs you can find in the forest."

"It's better for you," said Renald, not bothering to repeat his reasons for objecting to magic herbs more than the forest.

"Oh, Renald!" said the magician impatiently. But as Renald did not withdraw the accusation, Malgis opened the volume. "Look!" he said.

The pages were of fine vellum, and his handwriting was spiky against them. He had never taken to the smooth round cursives Bishop Alcuin taught in the king's court. The book had come open to a spell of disguisement, calling chiefly for walnut juice.

Renald glanced at it, and opened his hand a little, as if conceding a point. "That one's not magic. Everyone knows it."

"If it's known it can't be magic?" said Malgis.

"You know what I mean!" said Renald. "Anyhow, that's that one, but the rest aren't like that."

"Not the point." Malgis turned over to a page of spiky directions for summoning someone from afar. The three of them looked stubbornly at one another, and then, as his cousins showed no signs of yielding, Malgis closed up the book. He traced the sharp ruby triangle on the cover with one hand, then locked his arms around the volume. "This is my book," he said. "Not demons. Not fairies. No fairy—no demon—gave it as a gift. No index at the back to tell anyone with wit enough to turn a page how to do whatever needs the doing. I—"

"You shouldn't be jealous of Astolf," Bradamant couldn't help putting in.

Malgis glanced at her from the corner of his eye, and a smile of delighted amusement came over his face, as he made ready to score a point.

"Your good English cousin, of course, agreed to give you *his* book?"

"No," she said truthfully.

"And his really isn't his. Fairy gold, people will tell you, and for all anyone can tell you, fairy books are much the same. Melt in the spring with the snows, if he isn't careful. What does he want with it?" Malgis sniffed. "A handsome, nice-tempered sort like that—he should find himself a good wife and settle down and get married. So should you," he added, turning the attack on Bradamant.

Renald jumped in. "Good advice. Try it on yourself, why don't you?"

Malgis stopped short, suddenly rigid with fury. He took a deep breath, and managed to sound amused again, as he said to Bradamant, "Wouldn't have me, would you?"

Bradamant looked at him in surprise. Malgis had always thought of her as Renald's-little-sister, and his, too, by extension, as he had no sisters of his own. Then she realized he was enjoying her startlement. "Wouldn't ask me, would you?" she replied.

Malgis hugged his book closer. "I made the pages, I bound the pages, I filled the pages, I gathered the simples for my spells myself, and I gathered the spells myself, too. It's no one's gift to give back. This is *my* book. I made it."

"Oh, you did?" said Renald. "Where'd you gather the spells, then? Didn't get them from the nutons or the giants or any such demons?"

"No!" said Malgis.

"No, they're not demons, or no, they didn't give you the spells?" said Bradamant quietly.

He glared at them both, glared just as fiercely at the inside and outside mouths of the cave, then opened the book, gently, so as to do no damage to the spine. He began to read aloud, in words his cousins did not understand.

Renald jumped to his feet, drawing his sword, and caught up his shield.

Bradamant did the same. White mountain and white fist caught what light there was in the cave and gleamed, one against the other, as they swung their shields in front of themselves. It took less than a moment, but inside that moment she found she had time to realize—and be surprised at it—that she did not know if she was drawing to protect Malgis against Renald, or to be the one herself who took his book by force.

But it hardly mattered. Renald showed no signs of ague this time. She would lose. And what would become of Renald—or her, either—if their fight went on long enough for Malgis to complete his spell? He sounded as angry as Renald looked, and she did not trust what any of her hot-tempered family would do in the course of a rage.

Renald feinted down and swung up at her head. She caught the blow on her shield. It rang oddly. He was striking with the flat of his sword, not the edge. Bradamant shifted her grip to do the same, and knew that she was angrier than she had known—and that when she had more time to think about it, she would be horrified and shamed, because she had not thought to blunt her attack in the same way in the first place. But there was no time for proper feelings just then. If he struck her unconscious, or wore her down to exhaustion with the pain of enough bruises, he would win as effectively as if he struck a more lethal blow.

Renald took the strokes on his shield, and chopped at her with a heavy blow that sent her staggering back a few steps.

Behind them, Malgis' voice went on methodically.

Renald let her take the second she needed to catch her balance.

The nuton woman leaped past them, swift as a hare, and darted through the cave mouth into the light beyond the ivy screen, her hat pulled low on her forehead to shield her eyes. Outside, she gave a shrill whistle.

Renald kept striking blows, fast and steady.

"Think he's a woodcutter," Bradamant thought resentfully, but her own pace matched him. Neither one could get a solid blow past the other's shield.

The air between them and Malgis was glowing faintly. It cast odd shadows and odd lights.

Bradamant stubbed her foot on an unevenness in the cave floor she had not seen in the dim, confusing light.

Renald tried to land a blow on her head, but missed. The flat of his sword fell heavily on her shoulder, knocking her toward Malgis.

She fell against the bright air in front of the magician. It was gelling. She sank into it, but it held her, and she did not fall. She caught her balance and surged at Renald again.

He was out of shape, panting for breath, and slowing. So was Bradamant. It seemed very odd.

Malgis was gasping, too, and his voice went suddenly higher in the chant, as fear came over him. The magic he was working there in the cave was not under his control.

The brightness in the hardening air grew brighter, and the cave darker—no, it was that the light from the cave mouth had gone. Couldn't be sunset—too early.

Bradamant's eyes met Renald's, and they slued around to face the cave mouth.

The giantess was creeping in, filling the arch and blocking off the daylight. The grim, bony features looked angry, and all the grimmer because of it, her rough, barky skin made rougher by the frowning lines. Then she was in, and up, stooping to keep from knocking her head against the top of the cave. She reached out a hand to each, batted their swords aside as if Bradamant and Renald were kittens trying to scratch, grabbed them, and flung them away, one to each side of the cave. The impact against the cave walls knocked the breath out of them, what little breath they'd had left by then anyway, and for the moment they could not move.

The weasel jumped out from behind the giantess and tried to bite Renald, but the sharp white teeth closed on his boot. The weasel yelped.

The giantess snapped her fingers, without looking, and the weasel either found itself a hole in the cave floor or a shadowed spot to hide in. At any rate, it vanished.

The giantess was battering on the hard, bright air between her and Malgis. He had fallen silent. He stood panting, swaying a little. Her fists sank into the brightness without sound and stuck there at each blow. She had to pull them out each time, as if fighting against quicksand. But with each blow her hands sank farther in.

Something cracked, sounding like thunder in so limited a space.

The brightness was gone. Fresh air began to blow in the cave. The giantess leaned forward and caught Malgis before he could fall. She took his book of magic out of his hands, closed it, and started to set it on the cave floor, but he gave a squeak of protest, and she tucked the closed volume into his arms. She held him upright while he caught his breath, but her face as she gazed down at him was still angry.

He sighed, and leaned against her.

When Renald could speak, he said once more, "Burn the book."

Bradamant shook her head. She did not feel up to finding words for argument.

The giantess gave Malgis a little push, shoving him toward Renald. He rocked with the force, but did not move. He looked around at all of them—the giantess, his cousins, and the nuton woman, standing in the mouth of the inner cave.

Bradamant wondered when the nuton had slipped back into the cave. Between her small size, and her gift for fading like a weasel into the shadows, it seemed as if she could go anywhere, and not be noticed by anyone, except, perhaps, another nuton, or a magician.

Malgis spoke, at last, to Bradamant. "'My domain.' It seems now it isn't, after all. I've had responsibilities here, and I don't know that I've done as well by them as I might—"

The nuton woman stood, watching him.

"—but it was better than I could have done by Aigremont. I'll tell you what—" But although he still seemed to be speaking to Bradamant, his eyes, now were fixed on the giantess. "—if the fairies want to take my book, they have to take me, too."

There was a moment's silence.

Renald said, "Malgis, they're demons."

"No," said Malgis.

"Whatever they are—you can't think that's any place for you. You're human. Humans weren't made for those lands. I don't care what you think they are, you know you aren't the same. You wouldn't even be you there, give it a while, in their land."

The giantess gave Malgis a push, this time toward Bradamant, but he still held his ground. She thought a moment more, then turned and went down on all fours to squeeze out of the cave. With the entrance blocked, the cave went dark. When she was through, and the dim light returned, there was just time to glimpse—the giant hand reached back inside, and Malgis, leaping forward with his book of magic clasped to him under one arm, caught hold with his free hand. The giant hand grasped his and pulled back. He jumped with it, flying out of the cave, and was gone. A shadow sped over the floor to the cave mouth after him—the weasel, probably, although it went too fast to be sure.

The nuton woman turned away and disappeared into the inner caves.

The wooden bowl of salad had broken, split by roots growing down with the force of seasons packed into seconds. There was no telling whether the plants had taken it as time to grow when the giantess broke open the wall of air, or earlier, when Malgis was setting his unruly spell.

The spell was still at work. The leafy stuff, lettuce and cress, lay scattered unchanged on the cave floor, but the roots—radish, carrot, and endive—bedded themselves through crevices in the stone and shot up stems and leaves. Feathery carrot tops nodded over the short, round radish leaves. The endives burgeoned momentarily with little blue chicory flowers, but there was no morning light in the cave, and the flowers closed up again into dry sticks as fast as they opened.

Bradamant, for lack of anything more useful to say, complained, "Can't grow things in a cave."

"Maybe the nutons will transplant them," said Renald.

"By starlight?" said Bradamant.

He shrugged. "Daylight's not a nuton's nature. They can't help it." He climbed to his feet, leaning against the limestone wall. "Are you hurt?" he said.

"No." Bradamant tried standing up, and found she could. "I'll have some good-sized bruises tomorrow. You?"

Renald nodded. He rubbed his hand over his eyes, as if only from weariness, not to brush away tears. He coughed, cleared his throat, and burst out, "He can't love that thing!"

"Looks as if he does," said Bradamant.

"She's not human! She's not even pretty!"

Bradamant was silent.

He said wryly, "I shouldn't have told him he ought to get married."

"Maybe you should have. Maybe he should."

He stared at her. "You don't mean that."

Bradamant hesitated. "Maybe he was jealous," she said. "You had Clarice. I had Roger. While they lived. All Malgis ever had was magic—and a limestone kingdom."

Renald thought about it, saying nothing.

They pushed their way through the vines and out into the open air. They had to stand still, blinking, while their eyes adjusted to the light.

Renald put his arm around Bradamant's shoulder, to support her, and because he needed the support himself.

When they could see, they started back along the forest path, their eyes down, to watch for stupid-stones.

Chapter 10
Logistilla's Book

The air over the Channel was turbulent, as usual. Bradamant bent low on the hippogriff's back, shielding her face in the soft white feathers of the eagle head. When they reached the coast of England, the wind quieted a little, and Bradamant was able to raise her head again and guide the hippogriff to follow the coastline to the mouth of the Thames, and the Thames upriver to London.

It was at that point that she began to worry. Cenwulf's banner was not flying at the Tower. There were many peaceful reasons for Cenwulf to be somewhere else. He might be in his Mercian castle of Tamworth. He might be on progress with his court through all the Mercian lands. Many crops spoiled too quickly once harvested to bring a king his due share if he sat in one spot too long, even one with Roman roads running to it, and a good large river to carry goods. A king who wanted to get all his taxes had to take to the roads himself and eat things where they grew. Riding the circuit, the king and the court could meet his nobles and their people. He could go hunting in the forests. He could judge arguments that had not been settled locally.

But she knew one dispute that she would not want the king to settle. What the king saw as a peaceful mission to recover stolen property might seem like an invasion to the people there.

Even warlike missions would not have to mean one particular sort of trouble. There might be quarrels with Essex, or Wessex, or Northumbria, or Wales.

From London, they headed north and west, following Watling Street.

Bradamant tried to convince herself she was only borrowing trouble. Astolf had made no trouble for Cenwulf. Cenwulf had no reason to think he would. Holding Astolf's precious book of magic hostage had been a precaution, not a necessity. Cenwulf thought the fairies had stolen the book. His own men had seen a woman in elf-green go flying out the window with it.

All the same, guess and gossip could be great busy-bodies. Suppose gossip said that she had been seen flying about on Astolf's hippogriff, going back and forth between Mercia and

France. That was like enough. Suppose gossip said Astolf had not looked quite as surprised as he should when the book was stolen? That was possible. Could Cenwulf reasonably have guessed that Astolf was working magic again? No, perhaps not. Could he have guessed that it was possible to stage a fairy theft? Probably not.

She did not feel content with her probabilities.

The hippogriff, catching her worries, flew still faster.

Sometimes she caught a glimpse of the sun, looking more like the full moon, through the layers of cloud. More often, it was hidden. In the even grey light, the red and gold trees beneath her looked like a flat surface, something tiled in mosaic.

At High Cross, Watling met the Fosse Way, running from Lincoln in the northeast to Bath in the southwest. The Roman conquest had gone much farther than the Fosse, on up to Scotland, but the ditches of the Fosse marked off the land they had held most securely.

The hippogriff could have stayed on the track of Watling, following it west to the crossing with Riknild Street, which cut directly to Lichfield, a few miles to the north. But he left the lines of the roads, to head over the woods, straight toward Astolf's lands.

Then they found themselves in a wind, blowing them along still faster, under the grey clouds. Even before they came in sight of the castle, while the trees still blocked their view of the ground, Bradamant knew there was something badly wrong. The clouds ahead of them and to the sides were coming to meet them. All round the compass, winds were blowing toward Astolf's castle.

Not natural.

Flying above the trees as she was, she could not see much of the ground ahead. Her first sight of the castle at Lichfield was the top of Astolf's star-tower.

It took a moment more for her to see that some of the clouds were not in the sky above and beyond the tower, but were curling up it from below. Clouds of smoke.

Oak walls were solid, and proof against a good many blows— but not against fire.

The hippogriff, responding to her fear, put on speed. She already knew what she would see as they flashed over the clearing—the dispirited clump of Astolf's servants outside the burning walls, huddled outside under guard, and beyond them the soldiers swarming into the courtyard and daring the flames to leap through the doors of the inner buildings. Already she knew where Astolf must be, if he was still alive. The way the winds were blowing, he had to be.

Someone had warned the archers to watch the skies. Arrows sped by her, but the collision of the winds over the castle made accuracy of aim impossible.

The hippogriff lurched and let out a screech as the winds tried to blow them down a funnel. But he steadied himself and kept going. One arrow hit him a stinging blow broadside on the belly and drew a screech of indignation, but did not wound him. The rest did not even come close.

Bradamant bent low on his back, trying not to let any of herself project out beyond the hippogriff into the quarreling winds. For a moment, she was guiding him with pressure from her hands and knees, but gave it up. He saw where she wanted to go and was aiming for it as straight as the winds would let him.

Then they were on the balcony of the star-tower. The hippogriff's hooves smashed open the wooden door. The hippogriff stumbled, collapsing into the stairwell beyond, too large to fit inside it and fall, but also too large to get clear and disentangle himself. Bradamant squirmed off, bumping her arms and legs against the walls and the hippogriff's wings in the process. He flapped, trying to fend off this attack, and too upset to realize it was a friend getting in the way.

Strong, hard quills slammed her against the wall with bruising force. There were feathers over her face. She couldn't breathe.

She jerked down, stooping, pressing herself against the wall, and got free of the wingfeathers. She could not get at the top of the stairs. The hippogriff was in the way.

She jumped across the stairwell, just clearing the railing, and grabbed for a post as she hit, to keep from rolling down.

The hippogriff, startled out of his own panic by the clatter, froze, and fixed one bright eye on her.

"Get in out of arrowshot, if you can." Bradamant said. "Turn around. Be ready to fly." She was sure he could understand that much. She was not sure if he could do it.

After a moment, his muscles eased. For a moment more, he was quiet, looking at the cramped space around him. Then he was moving, squeezing to shelter himself inside.

Bradamant headed down the stairs, one hand on the wall, and one on the railing. She wanted to run, but there was hardly any light, after the first turning brought her into the shadow of the stairs above. Arriving in a heap at the bottom of the tower would not be of any use. She went as fast as she could, which was slowly, feeling for the steps. She knew she had reached the bottom when she bumped into a door she could not see. The blow set off a nosebleed, but she was too glad to be at the bottom and too impatient to be through the door to care.

She could not find the handle. She wasted no time feeling about for it, but drew her sword, set her shoulder, and burst into the room.

Astolf had his book of magic open, held with some difficulty in one arm. The other hand held a bloody sword.

He jumped at the crash of her entry. With a shout, he swung around to face the newcomer. He started to swing his sword up, but then stopped, without relaxing, as he saw it was Bradamant.

Lady Sylvia sprawled on the floor beside the doorway. A shield lay beside her, but she had not had time to put on armor. She had been struck on the head, and the skull had cracked open. She lay facedown in a puddle of blood, and it would have been hard to recognize her, except by her size, and the bundle of keys at her waist. Beside her lay a soldier in armor, bloody from injuries to the neck, in the gap between mailshirt and helmet, both front and back.

"I couldn't make it rain," said Astolf dully.

She would have stared at him, but she heard purposeful thuds from the other side of the barred door. Instead, she started toward Lady Sylvia, to see if, in spite of appearances, there was any life in her. Astolf shook his head, but she did not trust his despair, and checked for herself. She did not find breath or heartbeat. She sniffled, wishing the nosebleed would stop, so that she could cry properly.

The door cracked against its bar.

Bradamant shoved herself erect, caught Astolf by the sleeve, and headed into the tower.

The bar was still holding, but the wall creaked where the nails that held the supports for the bar were coming loose.

She slammed the tower door against the view. "Is there a bar on this side?" she demanded, groping in the dark for something to delay the pursuit further.

"Think so." Astolf touched her shoulder to move her aside. Leaning against the door, he said a quick charm. He said another, and the stairwell lit up—there were bits of carbuncle set into the walls, and they shone like fire. He looked doubtfully at them, and at the door, and at Bradamant. "Should hold."

They charged up the stairs. When they were halfway up, they were puffing, and started to slow down. But by then Cenwulf's soldiers were into the study and battering on the door into the tower. Bradamant used her hands to help, running up crouched on all fours, and kept going at speed. Astolf could not go as quickly, grappling with his book of magic, but he reached the top only a little after her.

At the top, the hippogriff was waiting silently.

They scrambled onto his back. Bradamant half expected him to crane his neck around to peer at them and screech out a protest at the sudden, double load. But he took a deep breath, tapped one hoof on the balcony floor, and leaped out with a powerful shove from his lion hindquarters. His wings snapped open. They plunged toward the fires below them. Then air filled the wings, and they were gliding, and in a moment more the wings began to beat, straining, and they were rising.

They just cleared the burning wall.

The wavering flames and gusts of hot air spoiled the archers' aim. Nothing came close.

When they had gone about a mile, the rain Astolf had tried so hard to call caught up with them. They were soaked in moments.

The hippogriff struggled on in the wind and wet for another mile or two, then dropped, so suddenly that Bradamant was frightened for a moment, thinking that his strength had given out. But then he spread his wings again, gliding downward, beat a few strokes to steady himself against the odd gusting of Astolf's turbulent winds, raised his wings once more, to cup a breeze beneath them, and settled into long grass and weeds. He stood, panting.

The two humans slid off his back, giving him room to take in deep breaths and stretch himself.

"Is there shelter here?" said Bradamant. Standing in a downpour was no way for even the weariest of hippogriffs to rest himself. She scrubbed her wet hand against her face, and realized she was not wiping off anything but water. Her nose had stopped bleeding, sometime during the flight.

The hippogriff pecked lightly at her side, and at Astolf's, and moved away from them. They followed him by the sound—it was impossible to see anything. The hippogriff, however, seemed to know by scent or touch the shape of where he was heading.

Then Bradamant found herself up against something solid, and nowhere to go. But she still heard the hippogriff, rasping against something ahead of her. She felt about and found a hole at her feet, and a slanting tunnel. It was not big enough for her to walk into, but presumably if there was just room for a hippogriff to squeeze through, there was plenty for a human. "Something underground," she reported to Astolf. He was only a pace behind her, but she had to raise her voice to be heard over the wind. She got down on her hands and knees and crawled in.

The way was thick with mud, and she kept snagging her knees on the bottom of her mailshirt. The metal made too stiff a fabric to be kilted up out of the way. Astolf's long wool robe could be hitched up in his belt to free his knees, but as he had only one hand free to crawl with, they made equally slow progress.

The rasping of the hippogriff's body against the tunnel stopped.

There was a large space just ahead.

Once into it, they left the mud behind. They were on a stone flooring, with stone walls about them. The walls were of large stones, neatly trimmed. The floor was of small stones, tiles, polished smooth. Above them, what seemed like a random collapse of planking had left a ceiling that held a space open, although the building as a whole had been lost beneath the ground. There was room for the hippogriff to stand, if he hung his head. The humans had to stoop or crouch.

It must be some old Roman's estate, Bradamant realized. The English, in a land of forests, had not yet mastered the more difficult skills of building in stone.

The tile floor was clammy, but a good deal more comfortable than mud or rain. Bradamant considered lying down and falling asleep immediately. She thought it would be easy enough. But there were other needs to attend to, as well. "Back in a moment," she told Astolf, and made the crawl back out through the tunnel. She took off her mailshirt, first, and slung it over a fragment of a pillar out of the way. She kept her helmet with her.

Outside, she wedged the helmet upside down in the earth, then moved away from the entrance for a convenient spot to relieve herself. When the helmet had filled with rainwater, she took it back inside, and gave some to the hippogriff. Astolf was kneeling, pressed up against him, grooming from feathers to hair to fur with his fingers, since he had no proper set of currycombs.

Bradamant still had a few strips of dried meat and a little wine. She put most of the meat on the floor for the hippogriff to peck up, keeping out a little for herself, and Astolf. She knelt beside him and gave him his share.

"Not hungry," he said, and handed it back. His voice still had that stunned absence of feeling.

"Eat it anyway," said Bradamant, and shoved it into his hand. She added what was left of the wine to what was left of the water in the helmet, and took several gulps. It seemed odd to be so wet outside and so thirsty inside. She passed the wine-and-water to Astolf and told him, "Drink."

Taking turns, they finished the wine-and-water, washing down the dryness of the meat. When it was gone, Astolf gave a sigh. The tenseness went out of his muscles. He sagged, leaning against her a little.

"How did Cenwulf find out?" said Bradamant, partly because she was curious, and partly to see if Astolf felt able to speak of his grief for his mother's death. Even if he could not do that much, she thought it would be better for him to speak to another human than to sit silent in the darkness until sleep overcame him.

"Don't know," said Astolf, a faint note of interest coming into his voice. "Wilfrid knew, but he wouldn't have told Cenwulf. The weather, maybe."

"What does weather have to do with it?"

"Good weather here this summer. Crops doing well. Too much rain to the south. Saw Cenwulf's reeve at a market fair, couple weeks back. He made a joke about the wizardry it took to guard the fields. Thought he was joking." He scowled at the memory. "Might have put ideas in Cenwulf's head."

"But you didn't use any magic on the weather—did you?"

"Just now."

"Not before, though?"

"No." He was silent again.

"I wondered if he knew your book could turn things invisible," she said, after a moment, and his interest sparked again.

"—could have figured out that it might not have been fairies stole it?" Astolf considered it. "Combination, maybe. That, and the weather, and maybe the reeve thought I'd been looking happier than I'd a right to."

Bradamant felt his weight shift a little. He was tightening his hold on the book.

"Can't see what I'd do without magic," he said quietly. "Not even an estate, now. What's there to do—go as a guard for your friend Isaac?"

"Marfisa enjoys it. It might be something to try," said Bradamant. "Or we could go to Uncle's court and serve as councillors."

"Live on his charity, you mean."

"No, I—"

"Should have fought Cenwulf for the kingdom when I had the chance," he interrupted bitterly.

"You wouldn't have liked it."

"No." He stood up, as far as the planking above let him. "Going out a moment." He hesitated, then handed his book of magic to Bradamant to hold for him. He stroked his hand along the hippogriff's back. "You?"

The hippogriff followed after him, and they filed into the tunnel. Astolf took Bradamant's helmet with him, to fill with rainwater again.

Bradamant meant to stay awake, in case he wanted to talk some more when he returned, but he was gone longer than she had been. The magical rainstorm must be letting up a bit. She stretched out, holding the book on top of her, and was asleep.

* * *

When she woke, it took her a moment to understand where she was, and why she was so cold and stiff. Once she had worked that out, she wondered why she was not cold all over, instead of underneath and on one side. She stirred. Something grumbled and whistled, and the warmth lifted from her and descended again.

She was lying snuggled against the hippogriff, and he had folded his wing over her.

She was not holding Astolf's book.

Now fully awake, she tried to slide out from under the hippogriff's wing, but she was too stiff.

The hippogriff raised his wing and opened one eye to take notice.

She stretched her arms and legs a little, and then a little more, and then was able to turn over and climb to her feet.

Astolf was asleep on the other side of the hippogriff, tucked under the other wing.

A little light filtered into the space from the tunnel. Now Bradamant could see that the tiles of the floor were inlaid with mosaics. The old Roman goddess, Venus, stood surrounded by doves. Beneath, her son Aeneas was pulling branches off a myrtle bush to make a wreath and had drawn back, astonished, because the myrtle boughs were bleeding.

She drank a little rainwater from her helmet, and stretched some more.

Astolf woke up, and looked about him, confused, then remembered as his eye met Bradamant's. "Morning," he said. His voice was not cheerful, but it was not as flat as it had been the day before. He slid out from the hippogriff's wing, carefully. Bradamant took his book again and held it while he stood.

He took it back and looked around the low room. When his eyes fell on the mosaic, he grimaced and turned away.

Bradamant remembered, then, that Astolf had been a myrtle once, transformed by a fairy queen, Logistilla's sister Alcina.

"Let's see where we are," she said.

They crawled out. The sun was not up yet. The sky was grey in the dawnlight. They were only a few yards away from a road.

The remains of a Roman wall ran alongside as far as a pillar that marked the crossroads, where another road came in from one side. Beyond it was a little cluster of houses. They were in the village of Wall, just south of Lichfield, where Watling Street was crossed by Riknild, from the north.

No one was up yet, except a village woman sitting on the pillar—no.

A villager would not be dressed in a grass-green robe, with no sign of the mud from the roads, Bradamant realized. And beside her Astolf had gone pale.

"Called her, didn't you?" he said.

"I didn't," Bradamant protested. "I couldn't—it would have to be a place of power."

"This *is* a place of power," said the fairy Logistilla, in the voice of one imparting instruction. "It is a crossroads. Now, you will tell me that the power of a crossroads is trivial, and so it may be—but I made that book, Astolf of England, and I need no human to tell me where it lies. I can meet you at a crossroads, if I choose. And you must choose which way to go."

"Do you have to take it?" said Bradamant. She had no real hope of keeping it for Astolf in their world, but she wanted to spare him a little more time, even if it was only seconds.

Logistilla considered her. "Look," she said, and made a gesture to Astolf to open the pages.

His hand shook as he traced the pattern on the cover that freed the volume. He opened it at random.

The page was blurry in front of their eyes. They looked up at Logistilla. She did not look as if she thought anything was wrong. They looked again, and by then the page was clear, but it had no spells on it. Instead, it was only words—words in alphabetical order, with definitions after them, as if anyone who knew to use the words needed to be told how.

"What is this?" Astolf demanded. "What good is it?"

"Spelling—spells," Logistilla said, musing a moment over the English words. "Speech was always at the heart of magic. They'll need word magic, one day or another, in England. Lichfield would be a good enough place for a dictionary to grow in a thousand years, if you let it."

"But you're not talking about magic," said Bradamant.

"A gentler magic, if you will have it so." Logistilla tapped the page. "Has no one told you that grammar is gramarye?"

"Grammar, the foundation of the trivium, which is the foundation of all learning," Astolf murmured. He looked at her uncertainly, as if he thought her words might mean something, in spite of jokes and punning.

All the same, Bradamant thought, even if Astolf agreed to define words as a gentle magic, it was hard to see the use of something so impractical. "Someone with a scribe's training might use something like that, once in a while," she argued, "but there aren't that many who can read, even with the schools Uncle's setting up, and parchment is too dear to—"

Logistilla shrugged. "Oberon has told you: that rough magic is drawing away from mortal lands." She looked at Astolf. "You have already had trouble working spells, have you not?"

He met her eyes for a moment, not bothering to answer. Then he closed the volume and closed his arms around it.

Logistilla turned her attention to the hippogriff. "What about you?"

The hippogriff hesitated, shifting his weight back and forth, from hooves to paws, paws to hooves. He shook his wings, rustling the feathers.

The grey light was growing stronger around them.

"He's not magic," said Bradamant doubtfully. "They breed them in the Riphaean Mountains."

"They may have done. It will not be possible much longer. A live hippogriff in your world will not be possible much longer."

The hippogriff eyed Astolf.

He set one hand on the hippogriff's neck. "Come on," he said, and started toward Logistilla.

"Not you, too!" said Bradamant. She tried desperately to think of anything to say that might stop him, or slow him down. "What will you turn into—a myrtle again?"

That brought him up short.

"Wouldn't do that to me, would you?" he asked.

Logistilla looked at the holly trees growing over the ruins of the Roman buildings. "I would not," she said. "But, then, my sister would not, either."

"Did before," Astolf said. "Turned me into a myrtle bush and took a new lover." He glanced at Bradamant as he said this, and his paleness gave way suddenly to a flush.

"No," said Logistilla. "You turned into a myrtle bush, and she took a new lover. It happened faster than it might to others, because you were enamored of her. The difference between us is that Alcina did not remind you that things change in Faerie before she let you land on those shores. I remind you of it now. But, then—you liked being a myrtle."

"That's impossible!" said Bradamant.

Astolf let go of the hippogriff to rub his beard. When he looked up he faced his cousin. "No, she's right. I liked—liked growing. Liked the peace. No, that's wrong. Almost wrong. _I_ liked…. There wasn't any _I_ in the myrtle, to like things, not to like things. Not much. Peaceful, just growing. Liked it until your Roger came along and started pulling off leaves and twigs. I bled. I hurt. I cared. I cared that I wasn't there. Wanted to be _I_" He shook his head. "Does that sound like anything anyone would understand?"

"I don't know," said Bradamant. "Roger," she added to herself, remembering.

"You make very good sense," Logistilla said.

He swung around to her. "But there won't be many heroes coming to your kingdom, now, will there? There wouldn't be anyone to hurt me." He held out his hand to Bradamant. "You come, too. You could have a dream of Roger there, until you changed. Couldn't she?"

"Yes," Logistilla said.

"I don't want to be a myrtle," said Bradamant.

"A cedar, I think," Logistilla corrected her. "But I cannot undertake that no one would come to break your branches, even without mortal heroes. There are imps and goblins full of mischief. There are dreamers who don't watch where they walk."

There was a cloud of fog on the other side of the markerstone, or perhaps Bradamant only imagined it. It was so faint, she could not be sure—a man-shaped cloud, it seemed to be, just beyond Logistilla. Roger stood on the other side of the pillar, holding out his hands to her, his eyes full of longing. Or she imagined it. She took a step backward. "No," she said to the cloud. "I'm sorry."

Astolf took a step forward, and another. He reached his book of magic up to Logistilla. Her hands touched his as she took it, and they stood that way a moment, hand to hand. He let go the book, stepped back, and bowed.

"I will remember you, Prince Astolf," said Logistilla.

"Thank you."

The hippogriff was teetering again. Astolf put his arms around his neck, stroking the feathers, hair, and fur. Then he walked back from him. "Live!" he said, and slapped him on the rump.

The wings snapped out as the hippogriff ran towards Logistilla and past her, rising into the air, east on Watling Street.

Glare flashed into their eyes. Beyond the hippogriff, the sun was rising. He was lost in its light as he rose into the air.

Logistilla stood up on the pillar, the book of magic tucked under one arm. She waved to them, then stepped off into the air. Walking upward, as if on a ray of the sun, she vanished like the hippogriff into the light.

A cock crew in the village, then another.

"Let's go," said Astolf. "Cenwulf will have to come back this way."

Bradamant took his arm. The idea of asking for breakfast in the village was tempting. Cenwulf had a large troop to get ready, and could hardly be on the road this early. But the villagers would be tempted to take Astolf prisoner, either to win the king's gold or for fear of punishment if they had let him go and failed to lie convincingly when asked.

They set off on foot, east along Watling a little way and then south, where Riknild began again, heading toward Wessex. The old roads generally ran straight, and that meant anyone on the road could be seen a long way off. They hurried along nervously, with a sense of itching in their shoulders. They kept looking behind them, until they had cleared the first rise on the southern track, and had the hill to hide them.

Astolf's magic thunderstorm had blown red and gold leaves off the trees. The autumn was not far along. The trees still seemed to be fully leaved, and many of them were green. But the road was paved with bright, wet leaves, sinking under their tread into a layer of mud. They shortened their steps, taking an easier pace.

"Will your people be all right?" Bradamant asked.

"Should be. Good at their work, and Cenwulf knows it. Going to be hard on the steward, though. Wilfrid's a friend." Astolf's face twisted as he added quietly, "He liked Mother."

"Does he speak French well?"

"Not well enough. Maybe Alcuin could find him something north around York, if he wants it. And the others—all right, I think. Saw to it they surrendered in good time."

"They would have fought for you."

"Probably—and then what? Their deaths, if they lost. Likely enough. More deaths later, if they'd held Cenwulf off. He'd have tried again—thought I had my book again, and the power to be a danger to his throne, and true enough, far as it goes. Couldn't have stopped him, once he thought that, without killing him, and if they'd managed that, would have won me the throne. Not likely, and not what I wanted. Thought the best chance all around was to get the others out, but not give myself up. He was too frightened of magic by then. Wouldn't have taken my submission."

"So you thought Cenwulf would try to burn you out, and you could have doused the fire with a rainstorm?"

Astolf nodded. "By then, would've had time to set the spell to go unseen. Could have slipped out in the confusion and got away. Hard on Mother, but I couldn't make her surrender with the others. Thought she might be right. He might not have taken her submission, either. She wouldn't try. I could have got both of us out unseen—but the rain kept holding off." Tears rolled down his face. "Running away would have been hard on her," he said, managing to keep his voice steady. "Maybe she would have said death in battle was better."

"I think she would," said Bradamant. "She was a brave woman."

Astolf shook his head. "Would have said it—even believed it, maybe. But she would have been wrong."

"That may be. But it was hers to decide."

He nodded, and went on crying as they walked, until his nose was stuffed up, and it was hard to breathe. He picked up some leaves that were free of mud and blew his nose into them, and by then he was done crying, for the time being.

After a while, Bradamant spotted an oak tree with a blobby orangey-yellow mass of sulfur shelf on the trunk. They stopped to slice the mushroom off. There were a few wolf-farts on the ground nearby—puffballs, the English called them, Astolf said. Bradamant shrugged, ignoring English sensibilities. "Good either way, if they're young." But when they bent down to try picking them, the little white globes popped open, letting out a cloud of yellow dust, and collapsed to nothing. The sulfur shelf, though, was fresh and sweet. They set off again, nibbling bits of the sweet, firm flesh. It would not give their bodies strength, but it was a pleasant taste, only a little cloying, and would keep their stomachs from grumbling. When they were far enough down the road to risk asking hospitality, it would be a welcome gift for the stew-pot.

"What makes you think Charlemagne needs my council?" Astolf said, when they had eaten enough to put their bellies more at ease. "—has councillors already."

"Not the same ones all the time," Bradamant replied. "He transfers them around. And that means there are places he has open somewhere or another, most of the time. And a king isn't the easiest person in the world to get along with."

Astolf gave a Humph, acknowledging his own troubles with kings.

"—so people leave, sometimes. There should be room for us, somewhere. Helping Alcuin set up schools for him might be the best for you, I think. It wouldn't be magic, but at least it would be books."

"Until Uncle quarrels with me," Astolf commented.

"That would be a good time to ask Marfisa to find some ship-board work."

Astolf was amused enough to forget his immediate troubles long enough to chuckle.

The sun went higher in the sky, but the air remained chilly.

A little past noon they came to a village. They would probably be seen going through in any case—especially if they tried to sneak around without being seen at all. And no horsemen had come galloping—or even trotting—down the road in search of them. They thought they could safely stop to ask for food.

Evidently, Cenwulf had decided it was a waste of resources to try to track down people who'd escaped by hippogriff. No doubt he would search for Astolf, but he would go at it more slowly. And they were hungry.

Astolf had with him some of the fine silver pennies from his father's mint. They were good anywhere. Soon the two were stuffing down chicken-and-mushroom stew, with honey-apple cake for dessert. They would have packages of both to carry away with them, and Bradamant asked for a roll of rags, besides. She expected to begin a month, sometime in the next few days.

They told the villagers the truth, approximately, explaining that they were on foot because the fairies had played a trick on them, taking away Astolf's hippogriff and his book of magic both, leaving them stranded on their way into France. It wasn't quite fair to Logistilla, but it would do. It would get back to Cenwulf, eventually, and it might—possibly—make him less afraid of Astolf. That would not help Astolf, particularly. He would be out of Mercia and out of England by then. But Cenwulf would do better by Mercia if he were not wasting his attention worrying about magical retribution.

When they had eaten, and washed off the worst of the dirt, and thanked the villagers, they set out again, feeling better able to face walking the rest of the day, and the day to come, and most of a third, depending on the condition of the road.

They were silent, at first. When they were out of sight of the village, Astolf said, "Are you assuming our roads lie together?"

"Yes. Don't they?"

"Would you want to marry me?"

Unlike Malgis, Astolf would not joke on such a matter. Yet he didn't sound as if it meant anything to him. "Do you want to?"

"My body aches me. I want to lie with anyone tonight—no, now, in the road." He kicked up a lump of mud and leaves. "—except the bedding might take away my longing," he added, with grim humor.

It made sense, of a sort. If they were together anyway, they could plight their troth and share a bed. Why not? It would be less lonely. He was not Roger, but to balance that, she was not

Alcina. She was not Lady Sylvia, either. She thought in some way it was grief for his mother more than interest in any woman that was speaking in Astolf now.

"I don't know if I want to," she said at last. "I don't think you know, either."

"That may be," he said flatly.

She thought some more. "Tonight—no. There'd be too many ghosts in the bed."

Astolf laughed. It sounded like real laughter, Bradamant noticed with surprise.

"What's the joke?"

"Thinking how awkward it would be if Cenwulf's sheriff came knocking at the door."

Bradamant laughed, too. "I'd like to see the expression on his face."

"—but not enough to risk the crowd on the pillow?"

"Not yet. Will you ask again—if you still feel like it?"

"Yes."

She wondered how much it mattered to her that he was not Roger, and how much it mattered to him that she was not eternally young and fair. Today, with a patch of cloud bright in her memory, beckoning to her from behind Logistilla, it seemed to matter a good deal. But Astolf was dear to her, and she had a feeling that her feeling would change. It was time.

They squelched along the muddy road. She felt in her pouch for the comforting weight of her leaf of fairy gold. The touch of cold iron would turn it to a withered skeleton, but so far she had kept it safe. She thought if their roads continued to run together, she would have it set in crystal and make a gift of it to Astolf. He would know how to appreciate its fragile solidity.

When they reached the Severn estuary, they would find shipping, and could buy passage into France.

Appendix

I

The Legends of Charlemagne

Of the three medieval classifications of legends, "the Matter of Britain" (King Arthur and his knights) and "the Matter of Rome" (the Trojan War and on into the Roman Empire) have both been enormously influential in modern fantasy. "The Matter of France" (King Charlemagne and his knights) is less well known. Charlemagne is better documented in history than Arthur or Agamemnon, but he, too, accumulated a vast legendry. Charlemagne's (historical) life was chronicled in the ninth century by Einhard, who had in fact been one of Charlemagne's officials. Einhard's *Vita Karoli* describes the battle of Roncesvaux briefly, concluding, "In this battle died Eggihard, who was in charge of the King's table, Anshelm, Count of the Palace and Roland [Hruodlandus], Lord of the Breton Marches, along with a great number of others." (It is available in English, in *Einhard and Notker the Stammerer: Two Lives of Charlemagne*, trans. Lewis Thorpe. London: Penguin Classics, 1969.) The name of Rotholandus as present with Charlemagne occurs in a document of 772, and a 790 coin includes the name of Rodlan. Einhard's single sentence and the two earlier mentions are all that is known to history of Count Roland.

(A note on the spelling of Roncesvaux and other names. Proper names going from one language to another suffer a good deal of variation and distortion, and also change going over time. The name which in modern French is usually spelled Roncesvaux appears in other texts variously as Roncesvalles, Roncesvalle, Roncesvales, or Roncesval. I prefer Roncesval, as the simplest. Moreover, the modern French *au* in this name—as in Renaud of Montauban, Maugis, and others—could appear in Old French as either *au* or *al*; this sound coming into English normally yielded *al*, as in such cognate modern French/English pairs as *faux/false*, or *baume/balm*. I have Anglicized the spellings of names in the story accordingly.)

Tradition and legend knew or invented a great deal more about Roland. Roland was not simply a leading warrior who died defending the king's rearguard in a retreat over the Pyrenees from Spain back to France, when the local Basques attacked. No, Roland was the king's nephew, his sister-son—on the model of Arthur's nephew Gawain or David's nephew Joab—the hot-tempered, sometimes rash, but always brave and loyal warrior, pre-eminent among the king's forces. The Roland of legend died defending the rearguard against an attack by the entire Spanish army.

The Spanish army, by the way, in Roland's time was Islamic. The Basques were Christian. The legend's rigorous division of the world into good-guy Christians and bad-guy Pagans is one of the reasons that more liberal modern writers have had difficulty in finding new stories in this material.

The historical Charlemagne may have been slightly more tolerant than the legendary one. His habit of carrying conversion by fire and sword into the territories he conquered was historical, but his officers were sometimes reluctant to kill heretics, as in the case of Bishop Felix of Urgel. And although the historicity of Charlemagne's councillor Isaac the Jew is somewhat doubtful, it is as a character in histories that he makes his appearance, not in the epics and chansons de geste that defined the legend.

The 11th century French epic, *La Chanson de Roland*, the first epic of Roland that has survived, shows the legend already well established. (A convenient English translation is that of Dorothy L. Sayers, *The Song of Roland*. Harmondsworth: Penguin Classics, 1957.)

The legend went on growing. With Charlemagne and Roland—as with Arthur and Gawain—the focus of the stories changed to include other knights. One such was Huon, the hero of the 12th century *Huon de Bordeaux* (author unknown), whose story introduced into the legends of Charlemagne the figure of Oberon (Auberon, derived from the German Alberich), the king of the fairies, mysterious yet benevolent. (It was translated into English by Sir John Bourchier as *Duke Huon of Burdeux* [1534]. The German poet C. M. Wieland's re-telling of the story, *Oberon* [1780, with revisions through 1796] was translated into English by no less than a president, John Quincy Adams. Before he became president, he served as ambassador to Germany, and he made his translation of Wieland during his ambassadorship

(1798-1801), to improve his German. Yet another version of the story was Carl Maria von Weber's opera *Oberon* [1876]. A modern re-telling of Huon's story, also emphasizing Oberon's role, is Andre Norton's *Huon of the Horn* [NY: Harcourt & Brace, 1951.] Huon's Oberon crossed over into English mythology as the King of Fairyland in Shakespeare's *A Midsummer's Night's Dream*, and has appeared as such in many English works.)

Another Carolingian hero was Renaud de Montauban, who appeared in the 12th century *Les Quatre Fils Aymon* (author unknown). Renaud and his brothers, the four sons of Duke Aymon, joined their uncle Bevis and cousin Maugis in a quarrel with Charlemagne that led them into armed rebellion, although in the end they were reconciled. (The story has not been translated recently; *Renaud of Montauban*, a slightly abridged version in modern English, by Robert Steele, was published in 1897.)

The legends of Charlemagne and his knights proceeded to cross the Alps into Italy, where they became popular, especially in three Renaissance epics, *Morgante Maggiore* by Luigi Pulci (1483), *Orlando Innamorato* (Roland in love) by Matteo Boiardo (1482-1483), and *Orlando Furioso* (Roland maddened) by Ludovico Ariosto (1532). (The *Morgante* and *Orlando Innamorato* have not been translated in full, although Leigh Hunt included summaries of them in his *Stories from the Italian Poets*, published in 1846. But *Orlando Furioso* has had two notable translations, in its own time by Sir John Harington [1591], and in ours by Barbara Reynolds [Harmondsworth: Penguin Classics, Vol. I, 1975; Vol. II, 1977.) In Cervantes' *Don Quixote* (1605-1616), the hero's madness grew from reading too many romances, especially the stories of Rinaldo (Renaud) in the *Orlandos*; Quixote found his own version of Rinaldo's helmet of Mambrino in his quest.

In the Italian epics, Renaud's family connections were expanded. He acquired a sister, Bradamant, herself one of the king's chief warriors. In addition to Bevis/Maugis, Renaud's father Duke Aymon now had two more brother/nephew pairs, King Otto of England/Duke Astolf, and Milo/Roland. This expansion of Aymon's family, however, is not entirely plausible. Milo in legend was poor, so poor that Charlemagne was enraged when the young man dared to marry his sister, and, in consequence, young Roland grew up in poverty. This poverty seems unlikely if his paternal uncles included two peers of the realm and a king of England. Moreover, the characters do not act as if they are all so closely related: Maugis is seen chiefly with Renaud; Astolf deals chiefly with Bradamant and Roland. In this story, accordingly, I have assumed that although Bevis and Aymon are brothers, the connection between Aymon's children and their cousins Roland and Astolf is not through Aymon, but through their mothers. (This in turn makes Charlemagne uncle to the whole clan—Maugis excepted—not just to Roland, an unorthodox arrangement, but not more so than the Italian changes.)

When I read Barbara Reynolds' translation of *Orlando Furioso*, it struck me that Ariosto's Bradamant is a delightful character—brave, loving, self-reliant, courteous, and stubbornly sure of her heart's desire. Ariosto wrote her in compliment to his patrons, the Estensi (the Este family), the rulers of the city of Ferrara, making them the descendants of Bradamant, and her husband Ruggiero (Roger), and she makes, indeed, an ancestress to be proud of.

It seemed a pity to me that there were no further adventures for her after the happy-temporarily-after (he dies young) of her marriage. So I set out to try to guess what some further adventures of Bradamant might have been, and this story is the result.

II

Modern Legends of Charlemagne

Some modern fantasy stories based on the Carolingian legends:

Castle of Iron, by L. Sprague de Camp and Fletcher Pratt (NY: Gnome Press, 1950). The second book (third story) in the "Incompleat Enchanter" series is set in the universe of *Orlando Furioso*.

Another of Charlemagne's legendary warriors was Holger Danske/Ogier the Dane. He entered into Danish legend as the sleeping hero who will awaken in time of need (a theme attached to many heroes in many cultures), and appears as such in one of Hans Christian Andersen's tales, "Holger Danske" (1843).

Poul Anderson's *Three Hearts and Three Lions* (Garden City: Doubleday, 1961) follows the further adventures of a wakened Holger.

Italo Calvino's novella, "The Non-Existent Knight," tells the adventures of a sentient suit of armor in Charlemagne's army. ("Il cavaliere inesistente" appeared in Calvino's collection *I nostri antenati* [Torino: Einaudi, 1960] and was translated into English by Archibald Colquhoun (*The Non-Existent Knight and the Cloven Viscount* [San Diego: Harcourt Brace Jovanovich, 1972].)

Andre Norton, besides her re-telling of the story of Huon, introduced Huon as a character in *Steel Magic* (Cleveland: World Publishing, 1965). Huon also made an appearance as Oberon's successor as the king of fairyland in the "Cold Iron" chapter of Kipling's *Rewards and Fairies* (London: Macmillan, 1910).

Gail van Asten's *Charlemagne's Champion* (NY: Ace Books, 1990) retells the battle of Roncesvaux with elements of the supernatural added; a sequel, *The Dark Sword's Lover* (NY: Ace Books, 1990), tells the story of Huon.

Judith Tarr's *His Majesty's Elephant* (San Diego: Jane Yolen Books, 1993), sets a fantasy in the court of the historical Charlemagne, and does not draw on characters from the romances.

III

Carolingian Heraldry

Charlemagne lived before the invention of formal heraldry, the systematic use of a single shield-design to identify its bearer (the design transferred to every shield the bearer used, as well as being worn on clothes as a tabard or surcoat—the literal "coat of arms"), and systematic rules for using, describing, and inheriting coats of arms. This systematic heraldry arose in the 12th century. But cultures and individuals had been using pictorial symbols to identify themselves long before. Once heraldry was invented, it seemed obvious to admirers of past heroes that any symbols associated with them must have been their coats-of-arms, and they freely invented the coat-of-arms for anyone (from Adam and Eve on) they thought ought to have had them.

Charlemagne used the fleur de lys (stylized lily flowers) as a symbol of royalty; the fleur de lys tipped his scepter, as it appeared on his seal. In the 13th century the fleur de lys began to be used regularly in the arms of the French kings, and legend backdated the origin of the royal fleur de lys to King Clovis (465-511). In Ariosto, the gold fleur de lys is especially Charlemagne's symbol. The eagle was also associated with Charlemagne, for two reasons, one looking ahead, and one back. When Charlemagne, King of the Franks, was crowned also as the Emperor of the Romans in 800, he began to use symbols associated with the Roman Empire. One symbol closely associated with the might of Rome was the eagle, as it appeared on the standards of the Roman legions. After Charlemagne, the German kings who gave the name of the Holy Roman Empire (neither holy, Roman, nor an empire, as the saying goes) to their territories, considered themselves the heirs of both Charlemagne and Rome. They called themselves Kaisers after the Caesars of Rome. (The German spelling reflects the original pronunciation of the name.) The double-headed eagle they used became attached to Charlemagne as well. Charlemagne's arms in legend became a black double-headed eagle on a gold field. Moreover, the imperial eagle was considered to go back even further than Rome, for the Romans considered themselves the descendants of the Trojans, through Aeneas of Troy. In mythology, as Ariosto recalled, the eagle was a symbol of Troy, because Jupiter in the form of an eagle stole the Trojan Prince Ganymede. Ariosto, in imitation of the shield made for the Greek Achilles by the smith-god (Greek Hephaestus; Roman Vulcan), asserted that the god made a shield for the Trojan Hector with a silver eagle on a blue field. In Ariosto, the right to bear a shield with Hector's eagle belongs to Roger, as the descendant of Hector of Troy. The popularity of Vergil's *Aeneid* made it popular in the Middle Ages for kingdoms to claim Trojan descent for themselves, no matter how implausibly. Thus, Charlemagne was the heir of the Roman Empire and through them the heir of the Trojans. Roger (not a king, but the ancestor in legend of the powerful Estensi Dukes) was the heir of Hector. The Britons were the heirs of Brutus (a Trojan prince found in the 12th century Geoffrey of Monmouth's *History of the Kings of Britain*, but unknown to Vergil or Homer). The Scandinavian gods were deified Trojan princes (also unknown to Vergil or Homer, but Troy was in Asia, and "Aesir" could just as well have meant "Asian," and that did well enough as proof, for Trojan descent was felt to be *very* desirable).

Roland: quarterly, red and white (silver). Although there are other arms associated with Roland, this was the blason Boiardo and Ariosto used. One legend (retold in Thomas Bulfinch's *Legends of Charlemagne*, 1863) explained that when Roland was a boy growing up in poverty, four of his friends gave him some of their own clothes (two had red and two white) so that he could have something to wear, and he commemorated their kindness in his choice of blazon. (D. R. Owen's *The Legend of Roland, A Pageant of the Middle Ages* [London: Phaidon, 1973] includes some 14th century illustrations of Roland with these arms.) In Boiardo and Ariosto, however, Roland's blason was explained as having formerly belonged to Almonte, a Calabrian invader. Roland killed him in battle and took his arms for his own.

Renald. Members of families sometimes signalled their kinship by bearing related arms. For this story, I have assigned to Renald of Montalban (white mountain) a white pile on a red field, to recall Roland's red-and-white.

Bradamant. In Ariosto, Bradamant is first seen riding with a plain white shield. But she has cedar trees embroidered on her surcoat, and when she is upset thinking that Roger does not love her, she adopts a new emblem, the stumps of felled cedar trees on a surcoat the color of faded leaves. In this story, I have assigned her a white fist (Bradamant implies "arm of adamant") on a red cedar on a white field.

Malgis of Aigremont (steep mountain). In this story, I have assigned Malgis a red pile on a white field.

Marfisa bears a gold phoenix on a green field with a gold border, according to Ariosto. According to Boiardo, she wore a green dragon spouting fire as her crest.

Astolf, the son of King Otto of England. England never had a King Otto, and England as a political unity did not exist in the time of the historical Charlemagne. But one of Charlemagne's contemporaries was Offa, King of the Mercians, and generally accepted as the Bretwalda (an Anglo-Saxon title meaning ruler of Britons) by the other Anglo-Saxon kings. Offa was probably the source for Otto, and so Otto has been portrayed here as corresponding approximately (although not precisely) to Offa of Mercia. His chief castle was at Lichfield. After his time, the town played little part in general history, although it entered literary history in the 18th century as the home-town of Dr. Johnson, critic, essayist, poet, novelist, and author of the first English dictionary. The traditional symbol of the Mercian kingdom was the saltire (criss-cross). According to Boiardo, Astolf's shield had golden leopards in a border of pearls. (The heraldic leopard is a lion "passant"—in a walking pose—staring out at the viewer. Ever since Richard I adopted a coat of arms of three leopards, leopards have been part of the arms of the ruler of Great Britain.) In this story I have assigned Astolf a Mercian saltire between two leopards on a blue field with a border of silver roundels.

The Anglo-Saxons kings did not, historically, trace their descent from Troy. But most of them, the kings of Mercia included, claimed to be descendents of Woden, the Germanic god equivalent to the Scandinavian Odin, who was later claimed as a Trojan prince.

Roger bears a silver eagle on a blue field as the heir of Hector (see the entry on Charlemagne for Trojan heraldry).

IV
Thanks

In the course of working on *Bradamant's Quest*, I often ran into odd questions that stumped me—questions of geography, mythology, linguistics, etymology, technology, physiology, etc. I would like to express my gratitude to many people who helped me find answers to my variegated queries: F. R. Akehurst (French), Bernard S. Bachrach (History), the late John W. Clark and Rafael Tilton (English), Dennis Lien and the others on the library's reference staff, Jane Tang (History of Medicine), and Peter S. Wells (Center for Ancient Studies) at the University of Minnesota; Ellen Kuhfeld (Bakken Museum); my late cousin and his wife, Jonathan A. and Helen T. Goldstein (History and Classics, and School of Religion) at the University of Iowa; Charles Ebell (History), at Central Michigan University; Miranda

Green (Centre for Advanced Welsh and Celtic Studies), at the University of Wales; D. R. Owen (French) at the University of St. Andrews; and the Office de Tourisme de Lyon. They are not, of course, responsible for errors or misinterpretations in the story.

I would also like to thank Eleanor Arnason, the late Anne Braude, P. C. Hodgell, Devra Langsam, Shirley Meech, Joyce Muskat, and the members of the Aaardvark and Rivendell writing groups for criticism and encouragement.

About the Author

Ruth Berman's work has appeared in many science fiction and fantasy magazines and anthologies, as well as in general, literary, and scholarly magazines and anthologies. She edited *Sissajig and Other Surprises* (a collection of the fantasy writings of Ruth Plumly Thompson, IWOC), *The Kerlan Awards in Children's Literature, 1975-2001* (Pogo Press), and *Dear Poppa: the World War II Berman Family Letters* (Minnesota Historical Society Press). She was one of the co-authors of *Autumn World*, a group novel (Stone Dragon Press).

www.ingramcontent.com/pod-product-compliance
Lightning Source LLC
Chambersburg PA
CBHW070529260626
47161CB00004B/1668